FIRES THAT DESTROY
HARRY WHITTINGTON

Black Lizard Books
Berkeley • 1988

**Black Lizard Books by
Harry Whittington:**

**A MOMENT TO PREY
FIRES THAT DESTROY
FORGIVE ME, KILLER
WEB OF MURDER**

Copyright © 1951 by Harry Whittington. Copyright renewed 1979
by Harry Whittington. **Fires That Destroy** is published by Black
Lizard Books, 833 Bancroft Way, Berkeley, CA 94710. Black Lizard
Books are distributed by Creative Arts Book Company.

Composition by QuadraType, San Francisco.

ISBN 0-88739-034-X
Library of Congress Catalog Card No. 86-71966

Manufactured in the United States of America.

I REMEMBER IT WELL

Harry Whittington

My writing life has been a blast. With all the fallout, fragmentation, frustration and free-falls known to man. I've careened around on heights I never dreamed of, and simmered in pits I wouldn't wish on my worst enemy, and survived. Maybe it's just that I forget quickly and forgive easily.

Looking back, I find it perhaps less than total extravaganza. It all seemed so great at the time: Doing what I wanted to do, living as I wanted to live, having the time of my life and being paid for it. I worked hard; nobody ever wrote and sold 150-odd novels in 20 years without working hard, but I loved what I was doing. I gave my level best on absolutely every piece of my published work, for one simple reason: I knew of no other way to sell what I wrote.

I've known some wonderful people in the writing racket. For some years, I lived in a loose-knit community of real, hard working writers—Day Keene, Gil Brewer, Bill Brannon, Talmage Powell, Robert Turner, Fred C. Davis. Out in Hollywood, Sid Fleischman and Mauri Grashin are friends, as were Fred C. Fox, Elwood Ullman. And via mail, Frank Gruber, Carl Hodges, Milt Ozaki. Death flailed that company of gallants—Gruber, Fox, Hodges, Ullman, Keene, Gil Brewer, Brannon, Fred Davis—all gone. Talmage Powell's inimitable stories appear in anthologies and magazines and, as of this writing, as I did in the wild and wonderful fifties when we all were young and pretty, I persist.

The fifties. The magic. Time of change. Crisis. The end of the pulps and the birth of the "original" paperbacks. In recent years critic-writers, Bill Pronzini, Christopher Geist, Michael Barson and Bill Crider have kindly referred to me as "king of the paperback pioneers." I didn't realize at the time I was a pioneer and I certainly didn't set out to be "king" of anything. I needed a fast-reporting, fast-paying market; the paperbacks provided this. I wrote eight, 10, 12 hours a day. Paperback editors bought and paid swiftly. We were good for each other.

The reason why I wrote and sold more than almost everybody else was that I was living on the edge of ruin, and I was naive.

James Cagney once said, "It's the naive people who become the true artists. First, they have to be naive enough to believe in themselves. Then, they must be naive enough to keep on trying, using their talent, in spite of any kind of discouragement or doublecross. Pay no attention to setbacks, not even know a setback when it smites. Money doesn't concern them."

Money concerned me. I'd never have dared become a full-time writer if I'd known in the forties that the critically acclaimed "authors" I admired from afar were college professors, ad men, lawyers, reporters, dogcatchers or politicians by day. Fewer than 500 people in the U.S. make their living from full-time free-lance writing. Since 1948, I've been precariously, one of fortune's 500. I persist.

Because, in 1948, I didn't know any better, I quit my government job of 16 years and leaped in, fully clothed, where only fools treaded water. I had a wife, two children and gimlet-eyed creditors standing at my shoulder. I had to write and I had to sell.

At that precise moment, the publishing world was being turned upside down by the Fawcett Publishing Company. When they lost a huge reprint paperback distribution client, they decided to do the unheard of, the insane. They published original novels at 25¢ a copy. Print order on each title: 250,000. They paid writers not by royalty but on print order. Foreign, movie and TV rights remained with the writer. They were insane. They were my kind of people. Bill Lengel, Dick Carroll and later, Walter Fultz. Elegant men. One hell of a publishing company.

Jim Quinn at HandiBooks; Graphic, Mauri Latzen of Star, and Avon were all swift-remitting markets once the spillgates broke open. I wrote and they bought. Once Sid

Fleischman wrote from Santa Monica: "Just came from the downtown newsstands. My God, Harry, you've taken them over."

It wasn't true. It just seemed true.

It wasn't all easy, not all beer and peanuts. There were rough times. You want dues paid?

I came to writing from a love of words. However, I wrote for at least 13 years before I truly learned to plot.

I admired extravagantly Scott Fitzgerald's writings all through the '30s when almost everyone else had forgotten him or, if they remembered, thought he had died, along with prosperity, in 1929. I couldn't afford to buy THE GREAT GATSBY, so I borrowed it over and over from the public library. I haunted used bookstores looking for old magazines in which Fitzgerald might appear.

I met a girl who bought for me—at one hell of an expense in the deepest Depression because they were out of print— all of Fitzgerald's books. I was so overcome with gratitude and joy and exultance that I married her. I still have her, and the books.

I spent at least seven years writing seriously and steadily before I sold anything. June 12, 1943, I sold a short-short story to United Features for $15. In the next couple years I sold them about 25 more 1000-worders, but it was five more years before I sold regularly. In that time, I worked for more than two years with a selfless, patient editor at Doubleday on a book they finally rejected. At this moment, Phoenix Press bought my first western novel, VENGEANCE VALLEY, July 10, 1946.

Using my navy GI bill, I studied writing. Suddenly the scales fell from my eyes. I understood plotting, emotional response, story structure. Fifteen years it took me to learn, but I knew. I could plot—forward, backwards, upside down. It was like being half-asleep and abruptly waking. Never again would I be stumped for plot idea or story line. From the moment I learned to plot, I was assaulted with ideas screaming, scratching and clawing for attention. For the next 20 years I sold everything I wrote. I enjoyed Cadillacs, Canoe cologne, cashmere, Hickey-Freeman jackets and charge accounts you would not believe.

I wrote suspense novels, contemporary romances, westerns, regional "backwoods" tales. People who wonder such things, wondered how I could crossover in these genres with such ease.

All very simple. I could write backwoods sagas because I came from mid-Florida when it was truly Kinnan-Rawlings territory. I could write "cattle-country" fiction because I lived in my teen years on a farm with cows. We had less than a hundred, but when you've known one cow, you've known a thousand. When you've hand-pumped ten-gallon tubs of water from a 100-foot well to fill those bellies, you know more than you need to know. I spent time on horseback, usually without a saddle. When I fell, as I frequently did, unsecured and fast-moving, that wonderful horse stopped in midstride and stood silently until I crawled back aboard. I didn't need to know a thousand horses, I just needed to love that one.

I never wrote westerns about "cowboys" or indians or "hold-up men." I wrote about people in a raw rugged land who loved, hated, feared and saw murder for what it was—murder. They got sick at the thought of using a gun. They used guns as you would in the same situation—as a last resort.

There was much talk in the fifties about the writers who "lived" their suspense stories. I didn't write that kind of suspense story anyway. I wrote about *people*, their insides, their desires, and fears and hurts and joys of achievement and loss. I wrote about love which flared white hot and persisted against all odds, because I was fool enough then to believe—and I still believe—that true love does persist, does not alter when it alteration finds. It may buckle in the middle sometimes, but it does not bend with the remover to remove.

If a character hurt in his guts, I wrote to make you *feel* how bad he hurt. I knew about emotional pain, which is the worst kind, and about physical pain. I was in two fights. In one, I got my front teeth smashed loose. In the other, overmatched, I was struck sharply in each temple by fists with third knuckle raised like a knot. When I wrote about pain, I knew what I was talking about. You don't have to die in a fire to write truly about arson.

How I came to write suspense stories is something

else. Bill Brannon, in Chicago, said he could sell all the suspense novelettes—about 10,000 words each—I could write.

Since I wanted only to be Scott Fitzgerald, with a touch of sardonic Maugham and J.P. McEvoy humor, I told Bill I hated suspense stories, never read them, and certainly couldn't write them. But I was in Chicago attending a writers' conference when I said that.

Having no idea what hellish jokes fate had stored up for me, I caught the bus home from Chicago—36 hours of leaving the driving to them. I was hemmed in against a window by a lady who looked like a giant-economy sized Nell Carter. In an attempt to escape, my mind plotted out the first suspense story I'd ever attempted. I got home on a Monday, wrote the story that night and mailed it the next day to Bill. That Friday I got a check from King Features Syndicate for $250. For at least 20 years I got small royalty checks from King Features on the 30 novelettes I did for them starting in 1949.

My path had been chosen for me. Fredric Pohl, who was an agent then, sold my first western novelette to Mammoth Western, "Find This Man With Bullets." Bill Brannon sold my suspense novel, SLAY RIDE FOR A LADY to Jim Quinn at Handibooks. I was on my way. I was less than a household name, but I was too busy, and having too much fun, to care. The people who read my books said I was a good writer, a damned good writer. How could I argue with that?

The New York *Times*, July 18, 1954: "Whittington does the best sheer story telling since the greatest pre-sex days of the detective pulps . . . YOU'LL DIE NEXT is a very short novel, which is just as well. I couldn't have held my breath any longer in this vigorous pursuit tale whose *plot* is too dexteriously twisted even to mention in a review."

Baby, I could *plot!*

From *Ellery Queen Mystery Magazine* (Paris Edition) 1958: "MAN IN THE SHADOW—Whittington's style is uncommonly lean and bare—it must have been difficult for the adapter to get his tone for French readers. But the impact is vigorous, the craftsmanship so smooth that one identifies with these characters, in their anxieties, their furies, their indignation, their rebelling against injustice, so we fully recommend this book to you."

And *Le Monde*, the largest newspaper of Paris, 1957: "With this novel, FRENZIE PASTORALE (*Desire in the Dust*), which compares favorably with Erskine Caldwell's best, Whittington asserts himself as one of the greats among American novelists." You can imagine how I blushed.

Nov. 4, 1955, the New York *Times:* "In THE HUMMING BOX, Whittington once again proves himself one of the most versatile and satisfactory creators of contemporary fiction—tightly told, recalling the best of early James M. Cain."

"SADDLE THE STORM, is one of the top six westerns of this year" said the *Saturday Review of Literature*, and the Western Writers of America voted SADDLE THE STORM number one of the 10 best paperback westerns of 1954.

Fifteen of my novels sold to motion pictures. Three television series were based on my books.

I was living high. One of the few people doing exactly what I wanted to do. In 1957, Warner Brothers hired me to write a screenplay from my western novel TROUBLE RIDES TALL for Gary Cooper. I couldn't write an adaptation that excited them. Finally, my option was dropped, the project became LAWMAN, a TV series starring John Russell and Peter Brown which ran about five years.

I had contracted the movie virus in Hollywood. I returned to Florida, wrote, produced and directed—and could not sell to a distributor—a horror film called FACE OF THE PHANTOM.

For the next eight years I could not produce or sell enough scripts to stay ahead of howling creditors. My agent decided I must do only nonfiction—things like "How I Made a Million in Florida Real Estate"—though I knew or cared nothing about the subject. He rejected out of hand the next five novels I submitted, then when I sold them myself, he demanded his ten percent because the books had once been in his office. He even wrote letters to editors threatening to sue if they bought my work except through him. I went to court and six months later I was free of him. But I had to write true confessions under my wife's name in order to keep my son in college during the long fight.

I signed, in 1964, to do a 60,000-word novel a month for a publisher under his house names. I was paid $1000. On the first of each month. I wrote one of these novels a month for 39 months. At the same time I was Robert Hart Davis, doing several 30,000-word novels for *Man-from-Uncle Magazine*. Strange things happened at Gold Medal. Walter Fultz called with the great news that my novel DON'T SPEAK TO STRANGE GIRLS had at first reporting sold 85 percent and was certain for immediate reprintings. Instead, nothing happened and Fawcett, which had been since 1950 like family, suddenly rejected everything I submitted. Walter Fultz even wrote a nice letter apologizing. The next thing Fawcett published by me was the novelization FALL OF THE ROMAN EMPIRE for which I "was the only writer for the job."

DESERT STAKEOUT went into six printings for Gold Medal once they did business with me again. CHARRO was reprinted five times.

The novel a month with the other work I was trying to do, plus the tensions and the debts, exhausted me. Emotionally. Mentally. Physically. I cried at weather reports. Then came the *coup de grace.* My new agent got me an assignment to do an original novel using the characters from the TV series MAN FROM UNCLE. The publisher had issued 30 of my novels and said he'd done well indeed. I'd always had royalty contracts from him. Now he wanted to pay $1500 for outright purchase of all rights.

What in hell had happened to me? Wasn't I the same writer who'd been giving the best he knew for 20 years? The agent advised me to accept. But he and the publisher knew what I didn't know. Mike Avallone had written the first *Man From Uncle* novel. It had sold at least a million copies and Mike was bleeding in rage.

So now it was my turn. I signed the contract. I wrote the book. I saw it on the Chicago *Tribune* paperback best seller list for *one full year* and I, who owed my shirt, made $1500 on a book that would easily have paid off all I owed and more.

I wanted to go on, pay no attention to setbacks, overlook discouragement or doublecross. With all my heart I wanted to, but I was too tired, too disappointed, too depleted.

So, sadly, I closed up shop. I still loved to write, but nobody cared, nobody wanted me. I figured if I were less than nothing to one of my most consistent publishers, I had come to a low place indeed. I had come by winding roads to the place where an agent and publisher conspired to use me for money the IRS wouldn't let them keep anyway.

I threw away every unsold script, put my books in storage. I quit. I asked for a job as an editor in the U.S. Dept. of Agriculture, and they hired me for Rural Electrification Administration.

I had reached the low place where writing lost its delight, the place where I refused to go on. No working writer knew more about plotting than I. Fifteen years it took me to learn. Twenty years I practiced. I was a damn good writer. I knew what made a scene real, what made a heart break or a reader respond. But I also knew nobody gave a damn.

For seven years, I worked in the government. I did sell three books in seven years because I felt *guilty* when I wasn't at my typewriter. What else was I? What else did I know?

In 1974, my wife—that same girl who bought out-of-print Scott Fitzgerald for me in 1935—got the name and address of literary agent Anita Diamant. Want a plot gimmick? She got Anita's address from Bill Brannon who'd sold my first suspense stories in 1947.

Mrs. Diamant arranged for me to become Ashley Carter. Since 1975, I've written the Falconhurst and Blackoaks novels, the antebellum slave stories of the Mandingo slaves done by Kyle Onstott and then Lance Horner.

Then I learned that during those seven years of exile, I hadn't been totally forgotten. Jean-Jacques Schleret, a French critic of Strasbourg, wrote to my Hollywood agent, Mauri Grashin, to learn when Whittington had died since there had been no Whittington suspense novel in France since 1968.

The *Magazine Litteraire* (Paris) wrote: "For the past 25 years, we in France have considered Whittington one of the masters of the *romain noir* in the second generation—after Hammett, Chandler, Cain of the first generation . . . his novel BRUTE IN BRASS is one of the finest of the genre ever written. . . ."

Gallimard, which had published my books in *Série Noire* now was reprinting them in *Carre Noir*. The French equivalent of the Mystery Writers of America, 813, Les Amis Du Crime, published a book devoted to my work.

The 813 and the Maison d'Andre Malraux invited Kathryn and me as Guest of Honor at the Fourth Festival of Suspense Novels and Films at Reims in Oct. 1982. Along with Evan Hunter, I was the first American writer to be invited to join 813. I was treated with such kindness and love and awe and attention that the entire celebration seems more dream than reality.

It was all an elegant and brilliant party. The French were the kindest hosts on earth. Jean-Jacques Schleret, Jean Paul Schweighaeuser, Rafael Sorin, Stephane Bourgoin, Francois Gerif and Robert Louit, all wrote glowingly of my work.

Back home in America Bill Crider, Bill Pronzini, Michael Barson and others praised my old suspense and western novels.

I wasn't dead after all.

This spontaneous outpouring of affection and warmth in France and here at home restored my old lost excitement and enthusiasms. It was like plodding for a long time in lonely night wind and coming suddenly upon a bright and festive place loud with love and laughter.

Rafael Sorin, writing in *Le Monde*, Paris: "(Whittington) . . . this prolific writer of more than 140 novels is largely unappreciated. He holds, nevertheless, an honorable position among that intermediate generation of the American suspense novel alongside David Goodis, Don Tracy and Wm. Campbell Gault. Even the most minor of Whittington's earliest narratives reread today does not fail to charm. Whittington, who acknowledges the influences of Cain, Fredric Davis and Day Keene is the most violent writer of this genre. His tomb of death can be the appliance freezer, alligators, mosquitoes carrying fatal virus. But his worst enemy is *la femme*. She who kills for money and devours those who succumb to her charms. . . . Whittington, who appeared pictured in his early books to be a rebellious young turk, arrives at Reims looking like a casting director's dream-ideal of the well-fed, successful TV lawyer. . . ."

The *West Coast Review of Books* in 1979 awarded Porgys to my RAMPAGE as "best contemporary novel" and PANAMA as "best historical novel based on fact." WHO'S WHO IN AMERICA decided to include me in their august pages. *Twentieth Century Crime & Suspense Writers* were most flattering as was *Twentieth Century Western Writers*.

Aroused by affection to optimism and resolution again, I could even remember the good which had accrued in the worst of times: The night at the Mystery Writers Award Dinner when I was introduced to Howard Browne, then executive editor at Mammoth Western. Howard greeted me, "My God, I'm glad to meet you. My chief editor Lila Shaffer says you're the most exciting new writer she's read. Better get a lot of material in to her fast. You've got a real fan there."

Or Harry Stephen Keeler, in his 80s and still selling his convoluted mysteries, writing in those years when sex in books was two passionate sighs, two loosened buttons and three asterisks: "Whittington is the only writer I know who can make a sex scene last for six pages without ever going out of bounds."

Or that most caring and selfless lady literary agent of Copenhagen who wrote, deeply troubled, in the midst of my 1960 battle to be free of an agent who admittedly planned to destroy me: "I cannot believe this man would risk losing your great talent for writing by his insensitive and selfish behavior. I have taken the liberty of writing to five New York agents (names and addresses enclosed) who each promise me they would welcome you, with sensitivity, caring and support, as a client."

It's been a wonderful life and I've met some wonderful people; it's been one hell of a roller-coaster ride.

Scott Fitzgerald once wrote: "There are no second acts in America." Maybe he was right. Maybe not. Maybe the trick is to hang in there—until after the intermission.

And, before we part, a few words about this book before you and the others selected for this classic-suspense-novel revival that constitutes the Black Lizard series.

Questions most often asked: Why did you write a particular novel, how long did it take to write it, where'd you get the idea for it and, where do you get your ideas?

First, my story germs are contracted differently than those of some of the leading practitioners of suspense and mystery, and even western, writing. Several stellar-performer-writers have averred on TV and other public dais that they start to write with no idea where they're going, or how their tale will resolve itself. One famous gentleman, writing for beginning writers, said he rewrote the ending of one book several times before making it come out right.

Despite the protestations of these best-selling writers, I personally find this lack of planning wasteful, unprofessional, and worst, even amateurish. Sometimes, I realize it's said to sound artistic. Still, it's much like setting out in a billion-dollar shuttle for outer space with no flight plan. Head for the moon, but if you land on Mars, what the hell? It's like a magician's walking on stage without knowing if he will draw rabbit or dove or anything at all out of his hat. In my world of writing at least, suspense is for the reader, not the writer. I can't believe bridges are built without minute preparations, or that Donald Trump okays a new tower which might turn out to look like the World Trade Center or Mr. Toad's Wild Ride at Disney World.

I usually start at the crisis, climax or dramatic denouement of my story, even if it's sparked by some unusual scene, character, situation or speculation. A story is not about "an innocent man framed by his own government" but how—with what special, carefully foreshadowed strength, skill, knowledge or character trait—he overcomes this terrifying situation. That "planting" and a preconceived "emotional effect" which will gratify, shock and involve the reader is truly what the novel is all about. Or, as Mickey Spillane said, "The first page sells the book being read, the last page sells the one you're writing."

Once a writer sets in his own mind "how" a story-line will be resolved, he is then freed to torment, tease, terrify or tantalize his audience. Alfred Hitchcock called this story core "the McGuffin," Harry Cohn of Columbia Pictures called it the "wiener." I call it the key, the complication factor, the gimmick.

Don't take my word for it. Let me quote Edgar Allan Poe who wrote, in reviewing Nathaniel Hawthorne's *Twice Told Tales:* "A skillful artist has constructed a tale. If wise, he has not fashioned his thoughts to accommodate his incidents but, having conceived, with deliberate care, a certain unique or SINGLE EFFECT (caps mine) to be brought out, he *then* (italics mine) invents such incidents, he then combines such effects as may best aid him in establishing this *preconceived* effect. If his initial sentence tend not to the outbringing of this effect, then he has failed in his first step. In the whole composition there should be no word written of which the tendency, direct or indirect, is not in the preestablished design. And by such means, and with such care and skill, a picture is at length painted which leaves in the mind of him who contemplates it with a kindred art, a sense of the fullest satisfaction. The idea of the tale has been presented unblemished, because undisturbed. . . ."

And I believe a good cabinet-maker can build a cabinet without rebuilding it forty-seven times. And I suggest he likely lays out his entire plan before he starts to build.

Having said this, I immediately stipulate that some of these writers who embark boldly with only nebulous idea, dramatic first scene or unusual character, have sold more books than Poe and I combined (and including Nathaniel Hawthorne). I still hold to my battered barricades. I still don't want to put myself in the untenable position where, when all else fails, I must resort to God in the machinery or "come to realize."

Anyhow, once I have worked out a "plot key" which will unlock my mystery, I know where I am going, even if I don't know how I will get there. I wish I could illustrate with examples of "plot keys" from these present novels without destroying your pleasure in them in advance, but I am sure you will discover them for yourself and, best of all, you won't be abandoned with the sense that the "outcome" was thrown in from left field. The climax will be carefully planted and foreshadowed, which is simply a matter of sweat and blood and hard work called "plotting."

French critics have noted that my heroes all are "disillusioned knights in rusted armor, often at battle with the very forces which employed them in the first place." I had no idea, as I wrote, that this was true, but in the face of so much evidence, I must concede. No one of my heroes is ever permitted, by his own disenchanted sanity, to believe in the sanity of the social "order" around him. For example, a nation in which an administration bases its policy on industrial/military complex greed, can talk blandly the insanity of "winning a nuclear war," insists upon sixteen thousand atomic warheads when three will be more than sufficient, and spend billions on it while refusing crumbs to dependent children and closing the Library of Congress at 5 P.M. daily; perhaps because that leadership got where it is by having never read more than three books in its combined life span, and wishing to provide every youth that same opportunity. My hero cannot put on the happy face. He is pushed to the place where he can trust only himself, even when he recognizes the impossible odds he faces. This does not stop him because he would rather die fighting than to surrender to greed, corruption and mean-heartedness, which places him as often at war with himself as with the uncompassionate and cynical power structure.

I often quoted FORGIVE ME, KILLER as answer to those who wanted to know how long it took me to write one of my suspense novels—and what delayed me?

With FORGIVE ME, KILLER, the answer is either four years or one month. I make no attempt to resolve the question, I simply state the facts: On March 8, 1952, I signed a contract with Fawcett Gold Medal for a novel (in outline) called MY BLOODY HANDS. Nothing went right. It was planned as a novel about a crooked cop named Mike Ballard who is gut-sick of corruption and his own smell of evil. He tries to atone for and redress the wrongs of his rotten city. But, as I wrote, I and Bill Lengel and Richard Carroll at Gold Medal saw it lacked something. One knew from the outset what the end would be. They had paid me a $1000 advance which they told me to keep and to get to work on something else.

By 1956, I was still stewing over that Mike Ballard novel and getting no answers. I accompanied a friend to a prison to interview an inmate for a *True Detective* article. When we arrived in late afternoon, we walked through a vaguely illumined, vast tomb-like auditorium where, far down front, the prison orchestra was rehearsing.

With this strange, eerie picture in mind, everything suddenly fell into place for the long abandoned novel: its mood, tempo, structure, complication gimmick, everything. Mike Ballard was no longer a disgusted cop but a man on the take and content with status quo. Don't ask me why, because I don't know, but when I returned home, I started anew and in about a month had finished the Mike Ballard novel. I now called it HELL CAN'T WAIT, Gold Medal called it BRUTE IN BRASS, the French publisher Gallimard called it VINGT-DEUX and many French critics called it "one of the best of the *romain noir* genre ever written."

Did I write FORGIVE ME, KILLER in four weeks, or did it take four long years? Whatever, I hope you find it intriguing.

FIRES THAT DESTROY was written to the classic mold of "character proof." (Becky Sharp's selfish ambition in VANITY FAIR is the best example). You establish your character with a strong (even obsessive) character trait and then prove that trait when in a crisis the character has the opportunity to be something more or less than the inner drive prodding him. When he behaves "in character" no matter the cost, his trait has been proved. I am betraying no secrets when I tell you my protagonist, Bernice, wanted above everything else to be regarded with the esteem and respect shown the loveliest of women. How she is given that attention and proves her trait is the story of this novel.

The hero—and he is one of my few truly unblemished heroes—in TICKET TO HELL is indeed the battered knight tilting against terrible odds and for no promise of reward. This does not stop him from fighting for what he wants—a truly disenchanted knight in rusted armor with only what he is inside, and an old long-lost love he cannot recover, to sustain him.

WEB OF MURDER, on the other hand, is one of those sweetly plotted novels Day Keene, Fred Davis and James

Cain used to concoct. We start the protagonist almost casually down the road to Hades and then follow him on every cruel twist and turn through increasing terror to the pit beyond hell. The reviewer who said WEB OF MURDER "proves that the death penalty may not be the worst punishment" exactly expressed the key to this novel. If you have half the fun reading it that I had writing it, we've got something going here.

The events in THE DEVIL WEARS WINGS are totally true and documented. This botched, bourbon-laced crime was one I wrote for editor Joe Corona at Fawcett's *True Detective*. But I could not get this tragic-comedy out of my mind, so I structured the true events enough to give them form, a beginning, middle, end and desired emotional effect.

The novel here titled A MOMENT TO PREY had a history almost as varied as its titles. When I wrote it, I called it NEVER FIND SANCTUARY, which Gold Medal changed to BACKWOODS TRAMP and which the publisher Gallimard, of Paris, called LE CHANT D'ALLIGATOR. It is one of my favorites. But I suppose a writer is like a proud parent: among his children he has none but favorites.

August 1986

Chapter One

Bernice stood at the head of the darkened stairs. A swath of light reached out almost to her feet from the doorway of Lloyd's bedroom. The downstairs foyer was brightly lighted and the shaded desk lamp was on over Bernice's typewriter in Lloyd's study. The rest of the house was in darkness. Below her at the foot of the wide stairs, Lloyd Deerman lay dead.

For the moment she was unable to move. Bernice stood and stared down at him. His head on its broken neck twisted back on his left shoulder, his unseeing eyes stared back up at her.

Her angular face was pale and her insides were tied in an icy knot. Her brown eyes behind thick-lensed glasses were dry and wide. Bernice was exhausted. She felt tired all over; so tired that she had to force herself toward the steps. Her legs trembled under her and she was afraid that she was going to fall.

The grandfather clock began to chime. The sound struck her like a fist in the small of her back. She stretched out her hand to steady herself against the newel post. She stood rigidly while the chimes reverberated eleven eternal times through the silent house.

Finally, when the sound was gone, she was able to move and she started down the stairs. Such a little thing, she thought. The sound of a clock and I'm paralyzed. How will I stand the rest of it?

She steadied herself against the wall, feeling the roughness of it against her hand, withdrawing from the sight of the twisted body below her. She descended each step singly, trying to delay until she could gather up enough courage to step around the dead man.

At the step above his head she stopped. She thought that he didn't even look like a man any more. His right leg

1

twisted oddly up under his body. He'd been big, weighing a hundred and ninety pounds. But he was bunched together now like a bundle of soiled clothes.

His hand slid off the step. Bernice caught her breath. He isn't dead, she thought. He isn't dead at all.

She bent down over him and held her head against his thick chest. She pressed her ear tightly into the crisp whiteness of his dress shirt. There was not even a tremor from his heart.

She straightened and placed her cheek close to his mouth. There was the odor of whisky. It was strong about him. But there was no warmth, no sign that he was breathing.

She stood up and backed away from the stairs. She kept looking at him, her teeth sunk into her underlip. She bumped against the foyer telephone on the end table.

Without taking her eyes from Lloyd's body, she lifted the telephone and pressed her hair away from her ear with the receiver. Her fingers were cold and stiff. Her hands shook so badly it was a full minute before Bernice could dial the doctor's familiar number.

Bernice stood, listening to the insistent buzz of the telephone across the wires. Finally a man's irritable voice answered. "Dr. Mundy's residence." He laid particular stress on the word "residence." "Dr. Mundy speaking."

"Hello," Bernice said. Her voice shook. "This is Bernice Harper, Doctor. I am Lloyd Deerman's secretary."

"Oh, yes, of course, Miss Harper." The doctor's voice lightened slightly. "What is it?"

"Mr. Deerman has fallen down the stairs. I wish you would hurry over. There may still be a chance to save him."

"Damn!" the doctor said. "I've warned him a hundred times! I'll be right over, Miss Harper. Don't try to move him. Don't even try to do anything for him. Just leave him alone. I'll call an ambulance from here."

"Yes, Doctor. Please hurry." She replaced the receiver.

She ran her long fingers through her brown hair, brushing it back from her high-cheeked face. It was brown, stringy hair, showing the crisp ends of futile curling, and she hated it.

She sat on the three-legged straight chair and stared at the body of her dead employer.

She was still sitting there when the doorbell rang. She stood up then and jabbed her fingers into her eyes. For a moment the room swam in the water that brimmed her eyelids, and comets and prisms burst behind her eyeballs.

Dabbing at her eyes with a damp handkerchief, Bernice went along the foyer to the thick front door. This was an old house, built in the late nineties, with gables, scrolls, and bay windows. It had been built to endure. And that's what it had done. Its narrow front porch opened on a wide busy cross street. It faced swank new apartment houses and backed against a drugstore, a delicatessen, and a pawnshop in buildings all erected since the First World War.

Bernice opened the door. It was a warm night, but the doctor was wearing a lightweight topcoat. It was turned up about his neck. He barely nodded and brushed past her into the foyer, digging a stethoscope from his black bag as he hurried.

He removed his topcoat and Bernice saw why he had worn it in the warm night. He was still wearing scuffed carpet slippers, and had stuffed his pajama shirt into his trousers and shrugged his suit coat over it. Bernice's mouth twisted in a wry grimace.

Dr. Mundy tossed his topcoat and hat on a straight chair. He was a gray-haired man of medium height. His ruddy face looked well fed. He wore pince-nez pinched across the bridge of his thin nose.

"He's dead," Mundy said. "I don't even have to touch him to know that. He would have to be. His neck is broken, and I imagine his spine is broken too, from the way he is sprawled."

He fixed his stethoscope and bent over Deerman's body.

Bernice sat on a straight chair. She heard the faint wailing of the ambulance sirens.

"Phew!" the doctor said. "He must have drunk half a bottle of whisky. He smells as if he'd rubbed it in his hair. And knowing him as I do, I wouldn't doubt that he had."

Bernice didn't answer. The doctor came over to her.

"I'm sorry, my dear," he said. He got a sedative from his

3

bag and gave it to her. "Get some water, Miss Harper, and take this. I'm afraid there's a lot ahead for you."

"More?" Bernice said. Her brown eyes flickered behind her thick lenses.

"The police will come with the ambulance."

"Police?"

"I explained that it was an accident. An emergency. That would be reported to the police. It's entirely routine, my dear. If it weren't for your overwrought condition, it shouldn't bother you too much. But I think it would be a good idea if you would go now and take the sedative. It'll quiet you."

The ambulance was screaming up the avenue. In a moment it would swing into the street before the house. The doctor flicked on the front porch light and left the foyer door standing open.

Bernice hesitated until the doctor looked at her again. He motioned with his head for her to leave the foyer. She nodded and went across the study into the private lavatory beyond it. The light fixed on the unfinished letter she had been transcribing made a painful glare that hurt behind her eyeballs like little demons jabbing with pins. She jerked her gaze away.

She closed the lavatory door behind her and then twisted the small lock. She crossed to the washbowl and with her thumb flipped open the paper container. She was going to sift it into the drain. To hell with a sedative. But glancing up, she met her face in the mirror. There was something in her eyes. It wasn't shock, and it wasn't fear, and it wasn't hysteria. Her hands began to shake.

She reached out for a glass, filled it with water, and poured the sedative out on her tongue. She drank the water, draining the glass.

She unlocked the door and opened it. She left the light burning and went back across the study to the foyer. Passing her desk, she again glanced at the letter, and again had to turn her head away.

Two ambulance attendants were standing in the hallway with Dr. Mundy. Their stretcher was still folded. One of the attendants was young and blond. He was smoking a cigarette. He glanced at Bernice and then turned back to Dr.

Mundy. The other man was young, too. He was short, stocky. He looked Bernice over carefully.

A third man, stringily built and cheaply clad, was talking on the telephone.

Dr. Mundy spoke to Bernice. "We're not going to move Lloyd's body. Obviously he's dead. The detective who followed the ambulance is making his report to police headquarters. There's nothing to do now but await the medical examiner. There are a few things you might do, Miss Harper, if you feel well enough."

"I'd rather be doing something than just sitting," Bernice said. The ambulance men looked at her again. She saw the stocky one glance appraisingly at the bundle Lloyd's body made on the floor. She felt a slow flush creeping upward from her throat.

"There are some calls to be made," Dr. Mundy said. "You are undoubtedly more familiar with them than I am. You'd better call Lloyd's partner, Joseph Sanders, and his lawyers and his family. By that time the police will be here and you can tell them what you know."

Bernice stared. The light glinted on the face of her glasses. "What I know?" Her voice rose slightly.

"Just keep calm, Bernice," Dr. Mundy said. "It's all routine. Naturally, the police will want to know what happened. Since you were the only one in the house, you'll have to tell them. Don't worry. As soon as the detective is through, why don't you start making those calls?"

"All right," Bernice said.

"We might as well pull out, Doc," the stocky driver said.

"I think it would be best if you stayed," Mundy answered. "You know more about these things than I do. But it seems to me the police will want a statement from you both. The time you arrived, the appearance of the body."

"Sure," the blond said. "The usual things. Shorty's just got a hot date with one of the babes from the clinic."

The detective replaced the telephone.

"O.K., Doc," he said. "They're sending Findlay over from the precinct. They notified the M.E.'s office. That don't leave us much to do but wait."

"Anyone for tennis?" the blond driver said. He grinned smugly.

Bernice backed away. She went to her study desk. She pressed a button on the memo pad and called Clive Behrens, Lloyd's lawyer.

He answered at once. Bernice could hear the music of a radio behind him, and shrill laughter.

"Hello," Bernice said. "Dr. Talbot Mundy has asked me to call you. This is Bernice Harper, Lloyd Deerman's secretary. Mr. Deerman is dead. He fell—"

"My God," Behrens said. "My Jesus God. All right, Bernice, I'm on my way over now."

He hung up, cutting off some woman's pealing laughter. Some woman at a party, Bernice thought. Some woman having a good time. Some woman with a man's arms around her. . . .

There was a longer wait at the next number Bernice called. At last a woman's sleepy, petulant voice answered.

"Mrs. Sanders?" Bernice said. "This is Bernice Harper, Lloyd Deerman's secretary. Could I speak to Mr. Sanders?"

"What do *you* want with him?" Mrs. Sanders inquired. "I'm sorry, Miss Harper, but Mr. Sanders isn't here this evening."

"Do you know where I could reach him?"

"My dear, I don't even know why you'd want to."

"Mrs. Sanders, Mr. Deerman is dead. He fell down the stairs. He's dead. It's very urgent."

"Oh. Oh, my dear. I—I am so sorry. I'll do what I can. I'll get in touch with Joe. I'm pretty certain I know where he is. I hope you'll forgive me. I had no idea—"

"Of course," Bernice said. "Of course you didn't."

She replaced the receiver and pressed another button on the memo pad. Her face remained set. The light from the desk lamp striking her glasses glinted, changing its pattern every time she moved her head.

This time the telephone rang almost twenty times. Finally a woman answered. "Hello?" There was panic in the voice. It was the tone of a woman who expected the worst when the telephone rang after nine o'clock at night. "Hello? This is Marsha Deerman. What is it, please?"

"Mrs. Deerman, this is Bernice Harper. I'm afraid I have bad news for you."

"Oh, my God!" Mrs. Deerman began to sob without

waiting to hear any more. Bernice heard her indrawn breathing, heard her speaking frantically to someone at the other end of the line. "Here, Francie, you take it. I—I can't stand to hear any more. It's about Lloyd."

"Hello." Now it was Lloyd's eighteen-year-old sister, Francie. Her voice quaked.

"Tell your mother that Lloyd is—dead," Bernice said. "It was an accident. He fell from the top of the stairs. Ask her if she wants to come over."

There was no answer. The telephone hummed in Bernice's ear. She was sure Francie had fainted. Then she heard a faint sob. It was another minute before Francie was able to speak.

"Of course," Francie said. "Of course. We'll both come. Thank you, Miss Harper."

Thank you, Miss Harper. Bernice's mouth tightened. She stood up.

The library door opened and a man stepped through it. He was like a gray shadow. At first, Bernice was sure it was an illusion formed by the light on her glasses. She even thought bitterly, It isn't the first time I've seen things when there was nothing there.

His voice was gray. It isn't the first time I've heard whispers, either, Bernice admitted. But now she saw that the little man was really there across the room. He said, "Miss Harper? I'm Detective Findlay. Fred Findlay. Dr. Mundy said I'd find you in here."

"Yes," Bernice said. "I'm Bernice Harper."

The gray man glided across the room. "Like to ask you a few questions," he said. "Dr. Mundy said it would be all right."

"Would you mind snapping on the overhead light?" Bernice said.

"Oh, no. Not at all." He pushed the button. The chandelier lights glowed. Bernice snapped off the desk lamp. That was better. Some of the pain in her temples subsided.

"You're Mr. Deerman's private secretary, is that right?" Findlay said.

"That's right," Bernice said.

"And *companion*?" Findlay was a shadow encroaching on her again.

"What do you mean?"

"Nothing. I don't mean anything. The doctor said you lived here in the house with Mr. Deerman. That's all."

"That's all," Bernice said.

"How old are you, Miss Harper?"

"I'm twenty-four," Bernice said.

"Really? Are you really twenty-four?"

"How old do I look?"

"Twenty-four. Twenty-four is fine. I know you're upset, Miss Harper." He wrote in his notebook. "What's your home address? Where do your folks live?"

She told him. He wrote again.

My folks, Bernice thought. They're going to love this. Especially mother. I can hear her now. I told you, Bernice. You were a good Christian girl. With a good job at Brennan's. You should have kept it. Think of the disgrace. Think of the neighbors.

"Your name is Bernice Harper. You're twenty-four and you were Lloyd Deerman's private secretary. And companion." Findlay was wandering around the room as he talked. "How many servants are there, Miss Harper?"

"Three. A cook, Mrs. Mason. Mr. Deerman's butler, Gilman. And a maid who did the housework."

"Where were they tonight, Miss Harper?"

"They were out," Bernice said.

He turned from inspecting the bookcases that lined three walls of the study. "They were out? All of them?"

"None lived in the house," Bernice replied. "They always left, every night. After their work was done."

"Oh? What time did they leave tonight?"

"I don't know. I was working. They don't usually say good night to me. By the time they're through here, they're tired and they just leave."

"You remember hearing any of them around in the house? Say after nine o'clock?"

"No. I was working. Here in the study. But I'm sure they were gone."

"Why would you be sure?"

Bernice stood up. "They work long hours, Mr. Findlay. They work hard. At the first chance they get, they leave."

"Suppose I told you that the cook was having trouble

8

with the stove? Suppose I told you I just talked to her in the kitchen?"

Bernice felt icy water in her veins. Her face flushed. She had to steady herself against the desk. For the moment she was stunned, exactly as she had been when the clock began to chime.

"I would say you're wrong," she said.

Findlay slid across the room. He stood directly in front of her. For the first time Bernice got a good look at that face. It was gray. But it was hewn from gray granite. Even the wrinkles pulled there by his age seemed agonizingly hacked in the flinty surface. His gray eyes were cold and humorless. When he spoke, his pale lips barely moved above his stained teeth. Bernice was afraid of him. She had never been so afraid of anyone in all her life. It was the first time she was consciously aware of being afraid of any human being. But she was afraid of this man. Afraid to stay alone in the room with him.

"Why would I try to trick you?" Findlay said.

"I know that the cook loved Mr. Deerman very much," Bernice replied. She was breathless. She hated herself, but knew she couldn't control it. "If she had heard him yell—as I heard him—she would have come running—as I did."

Findlay nodded. "All right, Miss Harper. I guess I chose the wrong team that time. So there was nobody in the house with Mr. Deerman but you. Nobody but you."

"Why'd you do that to me?" Bernice whispered.

"I have a job to do, Miss Harper. I'm a man getting on in years. Not married. Never married. Never did. A man gets to be my age, he's got to have something. I've got my job. I guess I know every trick there is to know, Miss Harper." He sighed. "Just as I know every dodge and every excuse and every lie that was ever tried."

"I'm not lying to you," Bernice said. "Why don't you wait until I do?"

"How old are you?" His soft voice broke across hers.

"I'm still twenty-four."

"Twenty-four." He wrote that down in his notebook again. He looked up at her, squinting, attempting to see beyond the barrier formed by the light glinting on her glasses. "Where were you when you heard him yell?"

9

"I was here. I was working here in the office. That's why I stay here in the house. Mr. Deerman liked to work at all hours. It was difficult to find anybody for a job like this."

"Was he easy to work for? Easy to get along with?"

Bernice looked at him. She moved her head a little. The light glinted. "No," she said. "No, he wasn't. Not at all."

He nodded. "Another score for you, Miss Harper." He looked slightly pained. "Don't make too perfect a score, will you, Miss Harper? I hope you won't. Too good is almost as bad as being all wrong. It takes away your amateur rating. Kind of makes a professional out of you. You can see how it might?"

Bernice lifted her head. Her mouth tightened. "I don't know what you're talking about," she stated. "And I think you're being rotten."

"If you think that, then you know what I'm talking about. Still. I'll have to give you another score. You aren't afraid to talk back."

"Should I be afraid to talk back to you?"

He shrugged. "There's no reason for you to be afraid of me. Unless you have a reason. Inside you." He smiled at her. "I'm just another policeman, miss. Trying to earn my salary."

Bernice shut her mouth in a tight line. Her hands on top of the desk were moist. She stared at the gray man and hated him. She hated him with all her soul. She had to control her breathing when she opened her mouth to speak. She was sure he could hear the erratic thud of her heart all the way across the desk.

"Let me alone," she said. "Let me alone."

He held up his hand. "Now, just string along like a good girl. Will you do that?"

Her mouth twisted. "You wouldn't believe me, anyway," she said. "Why should I?"

He met her eyes. "Believe me," he said. "Just believe me. You should."

Findlay's head lifted at the sound of the door opening behind him. But he continued to look at her. He said, "Do you have any idea, Miss Harper, how difficult it is for a man to kill himself by falling down a stairway?"

She was staring over his shoulder. Her breath sighed out of her. "Dr. Mundy!" she whispered.

Findlay turned and leaned against the desk.

"Why don't you tell her, Dr. Mundy?" Findlay said. "You tell her. Tell her how much easier it is for a man to break his neck when he's been—pushed."

Dr. Mundy closed the door behind him, The hallway was crowded now. Bernice listened to the chatter. She wished she were out there, even facing the reporters.

She watched Dr. Mundy cross the room.

He answered Findlay. "Because I don't agree with you, Mr. Findlay. My mind isn't on murder all the time. I sincerely believe my patient tripped at the head of those stairs, fell, and died from injuries sustained in that fall."

Findlay's brows went up. He jotted down a note. Bernice stared at the notebook, wondering what he'd written.

"Why?" Findlay said. "Why do you think that?"

"My patient was blind," Dr. Mundy answered. "He had been since childhood."

"Oh," said Findlay. "Oh. I see."

"Yes," Mundy said. "He was obstinate and perverse about his affliction. He was very independent. He had been repeatedly warned about trying to navigate those stairs alone."

"That makes a difference, all right," Findlay said at last.

Bernice looked at him. His voice was different. But there wasn't the slightest change in the granite set of his face. And he wasn't looking at Mundy. He was still staring at her.

Bernice shivered.

"Well, you've built up quite a score. Quite a score," Findlay told her. He looked at the doctor. His voice was sardonic. "You mind if I ask you a couple more questions?"

Mundy flushed. "I'm sorry," he said. "I was only trying to help."

"You have helped. I didn't know Deerman was blind."

"His family is here," Mundy said. "Maybe you'd like to question them?"

"Yes. Ask them in, will you?" Findlay looked at the doctor. He waited until Mundy nodded finally and withdrew from the room. He faced Bernice again. "I see there's a row of account books on that shelf behind you, Miss Harper. Right behind you. One of them is missing. There's a dusty

11

place. Obviously, it hasn't been moved—or dusted—recently. I don't see it on your desk. I don't see it in the room. Could you say where the book is?"

Bernice's smile was almost smug. "I don't like to make too good a score," she said. Anger gave her voice an edge. "But there are several books missing. Look around, you'll see."

"Yes, I saw. It's just that I wasn't interested. Now, about the account book?"

"It's been sent with the others," Bernice said. "It's being re-covered. Mr. Deerman is—he was very particular about his books. He liked the bindings new and serviceable."

Findlay nodded. "All right, Miss Harper. Thank you. Now, what lights were on in the house? Do you remember?"

Bernice nodded. "There was this desk light. The foyer was lighted. And there was one light in Mr. Deerman's bedroom. Upstairs."

"There was? How do you know?"

"I looked up!" she snapped. "I saw it burning! It's directly across the hall from the stairs. Anyone could see it!"

He held up his hand again. "You're about to graduate, Miss Harper. Just string along with a dirty-minded old man with a job to do. Will you? What about your relationship with Deerman? Where did it begin? How? Why?"

"What does it matter?" Bernice whispered. "Why do you care how we met, and where?"

"Just string along, Miss Harper," he said. "You have a good score. You can afford to."

Chapter Two

How did she meet Lloyd Deerman? And where? Bernice looked at the detective.

She hated him. She began to talk, telling him only polite and pointless lies. But inside her mind, behind the barrier of those thick-lensed glasses, Bernice was thinking bitterly, How did it begin, Mr. Findlay?

It must have begun in my mother's womb. Would you be shocked if I said that aloud to you, Mr. Findlay? Of course that's where it began. If you knew anything about genetics, you'd know that. You'd know about dyes and hair texture and tooth structure. You'd know two ugly people may be parents to a lovely child, their features blending into a pleasing whole. Or it can work the other way. Two nice-looking parents. Living up in the Bronx. Working hard. The wife going to church and gossiping about her neighbors all week. An ordinary woman. And the husband, drinking a little, looking longingly at the prettier, younger women. Their child is born. The first few years she has rickets, scarlet fever, and the mumps. When she started to kindergarten at five, they found out she has astigmatism. They put glasses on her and she wore them every waking moment. Sure, that's where it began, Mr. Findlay.

She looked at him. When did it begin? It must have begun the first time some woman looked at Bernice and said, "Isn't she a h-o-m-e-l-y little thing?"

She breathed deeply. She never learned to wear clothes correctly because there was never money enough for pretty clothes. Lack of money haunted her childhood. Some people can take a thing like that. Not Bernice. She grew up determined to have all the things she'd been denied. Someday she was going to be appreciated. Treated the way lovely girls were treated.

Personality is something you have to develop, Mr. Findlay. Or would you know? Or would you care? If you don't get a chance to joke with the boys because you're working all the time, you certainly don't learn how to joke with them, do you? But on the other hand, that doesn't make you any less starved for attention, does it? You become indrawn, secretive. When people did try to be nice, you snapped at them, and snarled like a vicious little lap dog.

She shook her head. You become sensitive. You become so sensitive that two people cannot whisper across the room without causing you to be ill. You're sure they're talking about you. You want to run. You spend your whole life running from people. And all the time all you want inside is to run toward them and find them waiting, smiling, and their arms outstretched. To hell with you, Mr. Findlay, that's how it began. And that's when it began. But I'd die before I'd say any of that to you.

13

Bernice could look at herself objectively. At twenty-four she was quite disenchanted. At fourteen she'd lain in bed, warm and excited, feeling the hot flow of blood throbbing through her when she thought about a boy, a boy's hands and a boy's arms and a boy's mouth. But she attended school and worked afternoons and evenings. She was always hurrying. They never looked at her. Or if they did, she was sharp-tongued, using her wits as defense against hurt. So they left her alone. She told herself that was what she wanted. But she knew better. She was lonely all the time.

She might even have been pretty, but her longing and her loneliness had made her unhappy, and it showed in her sharp, bitter face.

Bernice remembered vividly how she'd graduated from high school, near the top of her class, but not at the top, sliding through unnoticed. Maybe six people clapped when they handed her her diploma. She paid her own way through business school. That seemed the quickest way to what she wanted. She learned typing and bookkeeping and shorthand. They got calls at the school. They sent Bernice dashing out to answer them. She was the best student at the business school. They told her so a dozen times. Over the telephone, they praised her to prospective employers.

Bernice's mouth twisted bitterly. Let other people chant about capability. Thick breasts straining at a cotton sweater, that counted. A simpering smile. Eyes a man could look into and get a pleasing reflection from—not the distorted fun-house view that you got from Bernice's thick lenses. It was six months before Bernice got a job at Brennan's. This was an outsized import-export clearing house. Bernice was lost among dozens of stenographers. Her looks were practically unimportant. Practically.

Wait, Mr. Findlay, Bernice thought, maybe I'm wrong. Maybe it began at Brennan's. At least, that's where Bernice learned to hate. She'd learned about tears and slights and hurts before. But at Brennan's she learned cold, hardknotted hatred.

She had been there three years, and was still in the outer office. She was in charge of the stenographers. But that didn't matter. It was the inner office that counted. The jobs in there paid good salaries, and there was a chance for advancement. You could go places at Brennan's once you were working inside those magic doors. How many times had they skipped her? You'd laugh, Mr. Findlay. You wouldn't even believe it. She tried to get another job. She wasn't getting what she wanted at Brennan's. But there was nothing else that paid as well as the job she had. So she stayed. And learned to hate.

One day she was working on a detailed report. It was such exacting work that it had been kicked down to Bernice. She kept working even when she was aware someone was standing before her desk.

The man before her desk coughed. She glanced up from the report she was transcribing. Then she saw that it was Al Brennan himself, and that another man stood slightly behind him. She flushed, feeling her face go hot. She sat back in her chair, punching at the bridge of her glasses to set them straight on her nose.

Brennan was a handsome man. He was almost fifty. Except that his blond hair was thinning out some, it had remained almost unchanged for the past thirty years. He wore loud clothes and liked to believe that no one thought him a day past thirty-five. That was the magic age to Al Brennan. Before that a man is uncouth, immature. But at thirty-five, if he's used his brain, he should know the facts of life. He should be sophisticated, disillusioned, and charming. Al Brennan would have used all those adjectives to describe himself.

"Bernice, this is Mr. Deerman. Mr. Lloyd Deerman, Bernice Harper."

Bernice looked at Deerman. A big athletic man with graying hair, high forehead, and full jowls, he dwarfed the dapper Brennan. He had a smile that made him look like a friendly St. Bernard.

Bernice smiled and nodded, putting out her hand. Brennan's mouth pulled down and he shook his head meaningly, motioning with his head at Deerman's dark glasses.

Bernice realized that the big man was blind.

"Mr. Deerman is an importer, Bernice. Deerman and Sanders. I know you've heard of them. We've handled their account for a good many years. We find we're being

15

robbed, Bernice. Mr. Deerman has consented to leave his firm and make a confidential investigation for us. While he's doing it, he's going to have a suite of offices with us. He'll need a private secretary. We've given the matter a lot of thought, Bernice, and we've chosen you."

Some of the core of hatred dissolved in Bernice. It hadn't been wasted, she thought, all these years. They've known I'm here, after all. They have seen that I can do the work and know the business.

"I'm sure we'll get along very well, Miss Harper," Lloyd Deerman said. He had a well-modulated voice.

"Oh, I'm sure you will," Brennan said. "Only, call her Bernice. Isn't that right, Bernice? And, Lloyd, not only can she do the work, but she's a real looker." He grinned and winked at Bernice. Such a wonderful joke between them. A joke on the blind man. "Right, Bernice?"

Bernice went cold. All the blood seeped out of her face, leaving it pale and taut. Her legs felt too weak to support her. And she knew how bitterly she hated Al Brennan.

And she hated herself. She hated herself because it was a joke to pawn her off as a looker on a man who couldn't see her!

Looking up, her eyes distended behind her glasses, she hated Lloyd Deerman, too. She hated him because he was blind, because he had come to Brennan's, because they made a joke of her before him. It was cruel enough to overlook the quality of her work. But she was used to that. She could stand it. But to be made the butt of a crude joke before a man who need never know whether she was lovely or plain was tactless and unnecessary.

Her voice trembled a little. She fought to control it. "I don't know," she said. "Maybe I couldn't do the work."

"Nonsense," Brennan said. "Of course you can do it."

"I'm sure you can," Deerman said, smiling beneath his dark glasses. "I've heard glowing reports about you. We'll get along famously. Working for a blind boss is like working for any other, Miss Harper, except that he isn't watching you every minute."

Laughter seemed indicated. Brennan laughed as though that were as good repartee as he'd ever encountered. And Bernice managed a sound for the blind man. A dry laugh.

They gave Lloyd Deerman a plush office, and Bernice had her own cubbyhole adjoining it.

They worked together well. But she didn't get over hating him. She never got over that tactless joke of Al Brennan's. Bernice wasn't one to forget or forgive her hurts. The longer they stayed in her mind, the more they became magnified. She couldn't forget that Lloyd Deerman had precipitated that latest hurt. She had to admit it probably was the last thing he would have done if he'd known. But that didn't make it any better. She spoke to him only when he asked her a direct question. She was sharp and curt with her answers.

Bernice made a discovery. In spite of the fact that he smiled easily, had amazing poise, and got around well even in strange surroundings, Lloyd Deerman lived in his own private hell. Life for him had always been dangerous and lonely. This didn't draw her toward him in the least. It made her hate him all the more. A leper doesn't welcome another leper in the world of the well.

On the afternoon of the third day, Deerman called her into his office and told her to sit down. She unfolded her stenographic pad and laid it on her knee.

"I suppose there's a lot going on in the outer offices, Miss Harper?" he said. She watched his mouth pull into his friendly smile.

"I suppose so."

"It must be like being in a convent, being in here while the world roars past in the outer offices, eh?"

"What do you mean?"

"Oh, I know you don't like it in here, Miss Harper. A young and lovely girl, you want to be out there with young people like yourself."

"I'm not young and lovely." Spots of color appeared in Bernice's cheeks. A tiny muscle made a ridge along the side of her taut chin.

He smiled, his large mouth showing even white teeth.

"All right," he teased. "You're old and ugly and decrepit."

"I'm perfectly pleased, working in here," she told him.

He smiled again. "Well, you certainly had me fooled. Is that what you were trying to do? Were you holding out for an increased salary?"

"No."

"I'll see if I can't get it for you. You're worth anything you can hold them up for. I'll see that you get it before I leave here. Is that better?"

"Thank you."

"All right, Bernice. It's just that I wanted to be friends with you. I'm not really so bad when you get to know me. Perhaps it's just that I'm strange to you. Why don't we talk it over? Let's clear out of here and go to some nice place for dinner and music, eh?"

I should be your seeing-eye dog now, Bernice thought bitterly. I'm bitch enough, but not for that. If she had other dates from the office, it might not be so bad. She wasn't going to have them smiling when she went out with a blind man.

"No. No, thank you," she said coldly.

"Is it another engagement?" Deerman said, smiling. "If that's it, why, maybe some other night?"

"No. It's no other engagement. I just cannot go. I'm sorry."

"Do you mind my asking why?"

"Yes. I mind."

He laughed. "You're a difficult girl to get to know, Bernice. But I like you. You do your work. And you keep me in my place. That's all, my dear. Good night."

He said nothing more about her going out with him for another week, and Bernice said as little to him as she could. It was bad enough to go to the washroom and have the simpering little beauties titter and ask her whether Mr. Deerman chased her around the office himself, or did he just send his seeing-eye dog and let him retrieve her?

Work piled up. They sent in extra stenographers. Deerman refused to deal with any of them except through Bernice. Now she did nothing but take his dictation and deal with the personnel. Even so, her days were twelve hours long.

It was ten o'clock one night before he finished dictating. He stood up, stretched, and yawned.

"I've some news for you, Bernice," he said. "I found out what your pay was. I was astonished. Shocked. Not only that you could live on that amount, but that you would con-

18

tinue working here for such a salary. You don't have to worry. When you get your pay check, you're going to find it has been doubled. And it'll stay that way even after I leave here."

Bernice looked at him, her mouth twisting. You want to bet? She managed to thank him. But she hated him. Would he have done this for her if he could have seen her? Brennan's had increased her pay not because of her at all, but because Lloyd had insisted.

"Now," he said, "I think I'm entitled to a slight reward."

"Do you?"

He turned toward her. His thick brows raised above the rims of his dark glasses. "Don't you? Aren't you going out to supper with me, after that? Don't you want to hear the sad story of my life? How I was born barefoot? I was a year old before I ever wore anything but knitted shoes. Why, I don't think I had a pair of leather shoes until I was two years old. Come on, Bernice. Smile at me. Let's go out and celebrate. What if I'm not Prince Charming? Suppose I do carry a cane with a white tip? I'm a big guy, Bernice. I tower over most men. I don't have to see them to know that. I can *feel* it."

"I suppose you can."

"All right, then. Come on, Bernice. Pretend. Pretend for one night that I'm charming and handsome."

"You are handsome." Her voice was flat.

"I know. People have told me so. My mother has told me. I want you to meet my mother sometime. She thinks I'm handsome. So, we'll go out. Two beautiful people. I know a place, Bernice. Supper for two."

"I'd rather not. Really, I have a headache."

"You don't like me, Bernice. You find me distasteful?"

I hate you, she thought. I can't help it. It isn't your fault. It isn't even my fault. It's just what you are, and what I am. And what the world is.

"No. Really. I tell you, it's only a headache."

"No, that won't do. Not this time. I'm a sensitive man, Bernice. With sight I might have been a heavyweight boxer, a star football player, a sea captain. Now, I speak before Congress, and at luncheons all over the country. But I know. They aren't even listening to what I say. They're

19

thinking, My God, the poor beggar is blind. I wonder how he even finds the toilet. It's got so that I shrink from people. But not from you, Bernice. Some chemistry, some alchemy makes itself felt inside me, and I know we are sympathetic—in some unexplainable way, attracted. It isn't just that I'm asking you to supper with me. If you don't go, I won't ask anyone else. Certainly, there are hundreds of simpering little fools who'll go out with me because I have money, no matter what I am. I don't want that. You're my kind, Bernice, and I want to be friends with you."

Will that do for a beginning, Mr. Findlay? Bernice thought.

The dinner had looked delicious and expensive. Bernice sat stiffly across the table from Deerman. She was unable to eat. She could feel the eyes on them, the pitying stares directed at Lloyd. She kept her gaze fixed on the lustrous white tablecloth.

Deerman handled himself so well it was difficult to believe he couldn't see the food on the plate before him. He liked to talk to Bernice and he kept up a steady attempt to amuse her. It was twenty minutes before her cold unresponsiveness dampened his high spirits. He had started out this evening pleased and excited at being with her. But now her silence became his silence. He ate silently and ordered Scotch. He began to drink before he'd finished his entree.

After supper, fortified by the Scotch, he tried again. His spirits soared and he didn't want to let the evening with Bernice end. He insisted that she go with him to a night club.

In the taxi he reached for her hand and told her that he was afraid he'd find a typewriter in it, or a shorthand pad.

Bernice tried to laugh so that he could hear her. But all she could think was that she hated him. Al Brennan's smiling face loomed between them, and Al Brennan's sweet voice laughed at them in the cab. "Call her Bernice, Lloyd. She's a real looker. She's a real looker. Call her Bernice, Lloyd. . . ."

The evening was a flop and by the time Lloyd took her home he was drunk. And the hell of it was, he told her, that when he had started out with her he hadn't even wanted to drink at all.

20

Of course, Deerman didn't arrive at work the next day. But Bernice was surprised when he didn't show up the following morning, either. Al Brennan called her into his office.

"You've handled this whole situation beautifully, Miss Harper," he told her. "You've shown us that you can handle the tough assignments. There ought to be a step up for you when Deerman leaves. Yes, there should indeed." He rambled on for a few minutes, then said, "You know, Miss McMillan retires on the twentieth. Somebody is going to replace her, Harper. Somebody is going to step into a mighty fine position. Some woman who has proved herself with the tough ones."

He smiled at her, a handsome man of fifty who liked to believe he was a handsome man of thirty-five. An irresistible man being nice because he wanted something from her. Bernice discovered at once what it was he wanted.

"We won't say any more about that job now, Bernice. Can't, as a matter of fact. Something has come up. Deerman is at home. Just plain under the weather. We want you to get over there, Bernice, and try to get him out of it. See if you can get some of the detail work done there at his place. You know what I want. I don't think anyone but you would be able to handle it, Bernice." He smiled at her again.

He gave her the address of the big old house where Lloyd Deerman lived alone up on the East Side. She went there in a taxi. The first thing she wondered when she saw the old building, lost among the shining new ones around it, was why they didn't demolish it. Age had only outmoded it.

She went inside. The dark lower corridor smelled musty, and her eyes jerked up the high, sharp-angled stairs with Deerman's guide railings along the wall and the inner side of the banisters.

Dr. Talbot Mundy met her in the library. He smiled.

"He's just drunk," Mundy said. "He goes along fine until something happens to hurt him—and he can take a lot! More than almost any other man I know. But when the hurts pile up, he starts drinking to forget. He's a man who shouldn't drink at all. And he's a man who'll walk across broken glass barefoot for one more drink after he has started. We try to keep liquor away from him. Even the

21

servants destroy it when they find it in the house. When he gets started with it, he has to run his cycle."

Bernice stayed until they got Deerman sobered up and through the shakes and the sickness that followed. All the time she was thinking that maybe Deerman would leave Brennan's soon and return to his own firm. Then she would get the promotion she deserved.

The next day Deerman returned to his office at Brennan's. He told her that he was winding up his job here and was returning to his own business.

"I want to take you along with me," he told her. "I'll double your new salary here, Bernice. I'm going to speak to Brennan. But I wanted to talk it over with you first."

Bernice shuddered. She would never make double her present salary even in the job Miss McMillan was vacating on the twentieth. But she wanted to see the last of Lloyd Deerman. Being nice to Lloyd was like tending an invalid. Sure, it was plain he was crazy about her. But he wasn't what she wanted. Maybe once she got Miss McMillan's job, Brennan's would appreciate her.

"Don't speak to Mr. Brennan," she told Lloyd. "I don't want you to."

"Why not?"

"I'm sorry, Mr. Deerman. I'd rather stay here."

He faced her, frowning. Finally he said, "If it's because I drink, Bernice, forget that part of it. Sure I drink. It's not pleasant to live as I have to, Bernice. And sometimes it gets the best of me. Sometimes I have to drink. It's my own damn business! I'm offering you almost two hundred a week, Bernice. How in God's name can you refuse that?"

"It's easy," she said. "I just don't want it."

She couldn't tell him that she wanted to be appreciated by people who could *see* her. She couldn't tell him about the pretty, stupid little bitches who had been promoted over her head in the last three years. It would mean something to her to have Miss McMillan's job. She would at last be where she should have been for a long time now. In a job like that, maybe she would meet the kind of man she wanted.

Bernice was in the washroom when Rita Baehrs came in. Rita was slender and willowy. She had full breasts for such

22

a slender girl, and she wore dresses that displayed her bosom ideally.

Rita smiled at Bernice's reflection wearily, exaggerating a yawn. She'd been born out West, she'd told Bernice, and had come East to get away from horses and men who smelled like horses, laughed like horses, and danced like horses. She'd been married twice. She was planning to start a national Divorcees Anonymous. "There must be some way that we can curb these foolish mistakes we women keep making," she told Bernice. Now, she sank down before the mirrors on the narrow bench. Her pretty shoulders slumped round. "You'd think I'd been out snatching a new husband, wouldn't you?" she said.

"Haven't you?" Bernice said.

"Lord, no. Look at the calendar, child. You know what day it is? It's the nineteenth, that's what it is. I was out all night long convincing Al Brennan that he doesn't look a day over thirty-five. Positively not a day over. The inflated old bag!"

Bernice felt a chill clamp down around her heart. Lassitude slid through her limbs, leaving her weak and unwholesome. She simply had to sit down. She sank loosely to the bench beside Rita.

The old voices, the old childlike crying screamed through her brain. I won't stand it. I won't stand it. I won't stand it. I'll die before I'll let them do it to me again. I won't stand it. I won't let them. They can't hurt me like this again.

"McMillan?" she whispered.

"Sure, McMillan," Rita said. "Somebody is going to get that job. Only now I know who that somebody is. Me. Rita Baehrs. Omaha girl makes good."

"But you—you've only been here—"

"A year? Sure. So what? I've got the body for it, haven't I? I've got what Al Brennan thinks every thirty-five-year-old man should want, haven't I? Those are my qualifications. And baby, they're good enough for Brennan. Today he announces to the staff that Miss Rita Baehrs—get that Miss—will replace Miss Jane McMillan as of the twentieth."

But Bernice wasn't even hearing the last of it. She knew that Rita was telling the whole truth. Rita had got that job with the only qualifications that mattered at all. What a fool

Bernice had been to believe Al Brennan! It only went to show you. Hope sprang eternal in the chest of a fool. Her face was straight and she managed to congratulate Rita. But inside she was weeping and screaming like a baby, and wishing to God that she were dead.

Bernice returned to Deerman's office. She waited until Deerman told her how badly he needed her because he could trust her.

"If you need me," Bernice said, "I'll go. I wanted you to know it wasn't simply the money."

His rugged face lighted up about the dark rims of his blackened glasses. For a moment Bernice was afraid he was going to fall on his knees and kiss the hem of her skirt or something.

When she moved from her mother's apartment to the Bronx, it was clear that Bernice was going to live in a world of luxury and sin. And what were the neighbors going to think?

"What are the neighbors going to think with?" Bernice demanded.

Deerman couldn't keep his hands off her. He tried, but when they were alone in the house his hands would close over hers, or his arm would go about her.

On the third day she brought him a letter to sign. He was standing beside his desk. It was as close as she had ever been to him, her thigh brushing the inner side of his leg. He pulled her close against him. She could feel the banging of his heart. And she had never realized there was such strength as there was in his big arms.

What was the matter with her? What was happening to her? She hated him, didn't she? What made her writhe under the pressure of his big hands? Why did she seem to be on fire, all hollow in her loins, and whisky-hot? The delicious flow of that warmth fused through her, and though she felt feverish, she quivered as if she were cold.

He pulled her in closer, holding her to him hard and tight so her body could feel his body. She tried to remain rigid in his arms. He pressed in against her. She could feel the heat from him, the strength of him, and the hardness of his muscles. His breath was hot and his mouth closed over hers.

24

Her breath quickened, her throat felt tight and dry. She was weak in her legs so she had to slump against him for support. Her hands were icy and bloodless, without strength to push him away. It all happened with frantic speed. It had never happened to her before, and she didn't even know what it was. She didn't know what was happening to her. Her head reeled, she thought she would faint. She was on fire, aching to thrust herself against him, needing to—and hating herself because she hated Lloyd.

She had never known such excitement as there was coursing through his body and making her body limp with the throbbing heat of it. She had to feel it, and she had to feel her own writhing need to respond. But she hated him, and she couldn't help hating him. The thought that it was Lloyd touching her made her shrivel up and set the vinegar to flowing in her veins, and her body went stiff against his.

When he released her, she almost fell. He stepped back away from her.

"Why do I care?" he said. "Why is it everybody wants what they can't have? Why do I want you so badly, Bernice, when I know you don't want me at all?"

One night a week later he called her on her extension of the telephone. He was in his bedroom. "Come up here, Bernice," he told her. "I need you. I can't stand this."

She went. She was in her pajamas and her bathrobe, and barefooted. And she went like that. She even considered walking in stark naked. It didn't matter. He couldn't see her. The whole damn thing was the worst kind of mockery. She wanted to be desired, but not like this.

She pushed open his bedroom door. He was sitting on the side of his bed. His pajama shirt was unbuttoned. His dark glasses were off. His face turned toward the door at the sound of its opening. For the first time she saw the whiteness of his naked, sightless eyes.

She caught her breath. He heard her. The smile died. His shoulders sagged. He turned from her and grabbed up a fifth of whisky. He poured himself a drink. He didn't spill a drop. In this house he was master. He could wait on himself, find anything he wanted.

"Where did you get that?" she demanded.

"What do you care where I got it?" he said. "What does anybody care?" He drained off the glass, poured another.

"Don't drink that!" she told him. "You know what will happen."

"Sure. I know. I'll drink myself to death, and who'll give a damn? Let me alone. Get out of here. I'm alone. That's the way it's got to be. That's the way I want it."

She went over, wrested the bottle from his hand, and smashed it across the radiator. Steam rose and the smell pervaded the room.

"Sleep in it!" she told him. "Sleep with it! Feel sorry for yourself!"

He twisted around and sprawled across the bed. A sob racked his thick, broad shoulders. Bernice walked slowly out of the room.

The next day he was all right. At nine o'clock he called her to help him down the stairs. They had breakfast together, the girl who wanted to be admired, and the man who wanted to be loved. The start of another beautiful day, Bernice thought bitterly.

They went to work in the study. Lloyd called to her and told her to bring him an account book from the shelf above her. She stood on a small ladder and lifted one of the books down. When she opened it she caught her breath. She bit down on her underlip and set the book quietly on her desk.

"It's the one marked 'Open Account'!" Lloyd snapped. "Can't anybody around this place find anything?"

She took the book he wanted to him and returned to the one on her desk. She opened it. It was hollowed. In it were ten stacks of money, secured with rubber bands. The least of them were hundred-dollar bills. She had no idea yet how much was there—many thousands. With the cover turned back, she stared.

Maybe it began there, she thought savagely. How's that for a beginning, Mr. Findlay?

Chapter Three

There was only one way for Bernice to have that money. It never occurred to her that she wasn't going to have it. She could have married Lloyd and had all his money. But at twenty-four, Bernice knew what she wanted. She knew she wanted only one thing. She wanted to be treated the way beautiful women are treated. Marrying Lloyd Deerman wouldn't get her that. Not even if she could have stomached the idea at all. A few knowing looks. A few smart laughs. Pity. That's what she'd get married to Lloyd.

She couldn't steal it. She knew better than that. Not even slowly. Not even a few dollars at a time. He would miss it. And that wasn't the way she wanted that money, anyhow. She wanted it all at once. That first night, she stood staring at the thick, tight stacks of money in the false-fronted account book. She wondered, Why does he keep this money hidden here? Why separate from his banking accounts?

Bernice felt she knew the answer to that, too. She made a careful, secret audit of his accounts. This money was nowhere itemized. It was free, apart from all his listed assets. No one knew he had it hidden. Blind and growing daily more suspicious and resentful, Lloyd mistrusted even the banks in the dark world in which he existed.

She remembered what Dr. Talbot Mundy had told her. "Many blind men are well adjusted, Bernice. They've reconciled themselves. Made their peace. Accepted their lot. They lead almost normal lives. Do carpentry, masonry, plumbing, and become business and professional leaders. Even Lloyd is highly successful. He has spoken to law, medical, and professional groups all over the country. But a strange thing has been happening to him. I don't know what it is, but I do know it's like a malignant growth. The best name I can find for it is simply resentment. When he was younger, Lloyd did everything in the world to prove he was as good blind as any two men who could see. He crossed busy streets alone. He remembered addresses.

27

He could leave my office and go downtown to a bar or a restaurant or even the offices of acquaintances, unaided. He began to be successful. The more successful he became, the more resentful he became. He had proved to himself and the world that he could conquer it without his eyes. Poor devil. He found out the reaction was: So what? More sincere men than one are beaten by that reaction to their merit.

"He has been steadily withdrawing into himself. Living alone in this old house until you came. Drinking himself unconscious. Alienating any who tried to help him. He wants to be accepted for himself and it has embittered him because he is not."

That first night she replaced the big book in its niche on the shelf. Her heart was pounding. Her fingers were bloodless and cold. She had to force herself to work.

By midnight, Lloyd was asleep. Bernice tiptoed down the stairs. She drew the blinds at the windows of the study, locked the foyer door. By the small shaded light over her desk she counted the money. There was over twenty-four thousand dollars.

At first she was disappointed. But only at first. She replaced the book again, turned off the lights, retraced her steps up to her bedroom. She was smiling. There was something perfect about that amount. Adequate. Almost inconspicuous. Easy to handle, hide, conceal. Yet enough to buy for herself what she wanted. Perfect.

She lay breathless and sweated on her pillow. Almost as she had in those nights when she'd dreamed of boys. She tried to tell herself that she just could not imagine any way that money could ever be hers.

But she knew she lied.

She knew the only way she could ever have it.

She had known it from the first moment.

She couldn't force her mind beyond that point. Not at first. Not for the first few nights. She would lie awake and think about that money. The things it would buy. The places it would take her. And then she would realize she was fatigued. Tired all over her body. Her mind would refuse to concentrate any more. And she would sleep. . . .

■   ■   ■

. . . And she would walk into a room. A room where inverted mushrooms were painted on the walls and ceilings and floors. Greens and reds and pink. There was something upsetting about the way they were painted. They stirred her. Upset her. Frightened her in a way that wasn't fright at all.

Attracted and repelled by the gaudy room, she started across it. There was Rita Baehrs before her. She wanted to hate Rita. Rita had taken Al Brennan to bed in order to get Jane McMillan's job. Rita had taken that job from Bernice. Bernice had a right to hate her. But Bernice smiled when she wanted to sneer. She hurried forward. And Rita smiled and came running toward Bernice. But in the center of the room there was a small bridge between them. It was made of white plaster. It spanned an odd-shaped pool of water. Red water. Blood-red water. At the bridge, Bernice stopped, shivering and cold. Across on the other side, Rita stopped too. Rita beckoned. Then Bernice saw that the girl on the other side of the blood-red pool wasn't Rita Baehrs at all.

It was she. It was Bernice. Only she was so lovely that she hadn't even recognized herself. She smiled and the lovely Bernice smiled back. She laughed. She began to laugh hysterically. The room shook with her laughter. Ripples spun around on the surface of the red pool. The gaudy mushrooms stretched and elongated and slithered on the wall like bright serpents. The room quavered and trembled as she laughed. She couldn't stop laughing. She could only go on laughing until she cried. The tears wet her cheeks, and she woke up laughing. . . .

When finally you admit that you are going to kill a man, your obsession takes over. You begin to plan how you can do it—and get away with it.

Bernice took her time. The weeks passed. Sometimes it seemed to her she wasn't planning at all. Sometimes she told herself it was just a joke. It was just something she thought about to make her life with Lloyd bearable.

But not a day passed that Bernice didn't count the money.

Lloyd himself suggested that she select from the library any books that seemed frayed or smudged and send them out to be rebound.

And so he set the day for his own execution.

He knew nothing about it, of course. It seemed to him that life had never been so fine between him and Bernice. The world might still be unfriendly, but Bernice pleased him. She spoke warmly to him. She was even responsive when he touched her, and she laughed at his jokes.

As far as she was concerned, he was already dead.

The bindery men called for the books. Bernice demanded to know the earliest possible date that they could expect to get the books back. The men were only clerks and had no idea. Lloyd was listening. He applauded Bernice. They called the office of the bookbinders and a date was set for the return of the books.

Good, Bernice thought. When they send them, I won't be here.

The night Lloyd was to die arrived.

Bernice had a fifth of good whisky locked in her study desk drawer. She'd bought an expensive, highly recommended brand.

At eight, Gilman, Lloyd's butler, said good night. He left through the front door. Bernice locked it after him.

There were two doors in the rear, and a side entrance that once had opened on the carriage drive. The drive had long ago been closed. The door was seldom used. Bernice merely checked it. She wanted only to be sure that it was bolted. Then she locked the two rear doors.

There was nothing unusual in this. She checked the doors and locked them every night. Only now, she was reasonably sure no one would walk in.

She went about the lower floor of the house slowly. She turned off all lights except the work lamp on her study desk. She pulled the shades, not tightly, but enough so that no one could see whether she was at her desk or not.

She inserted letterhead paper, carbon, and second sheet, and transcribed maybe a third of a letter Lloyd had dictated that afternoon.

Only then did she remove the false-fronted account book from the shelf. She looked once at the money inside it. She felt the breath seep across her dry lips.

This was the weak part of the whole business, she told herself bitterly. She had to get that book out of the house.

30

She had not dared move it too soon, for she had no way of knowing when Lloyd would check on that book. She had never seen him even go near it, but that didn't mean that he wasn't acutely aware of it. She had learned that Lloyd had a sense for things that people who see never develop. This was the first possible moment she could dare move the book.

She had discarded a dozen plans. She had thought of wrapping it securely and addressing it to herself at her mother's home in the Bronx. There were a lot of holes in that. Her mother might very well forward it right back here. My lovely mother, Bernice thought. Besides, detectives had such damnable ways of walking and walking and walking. If one of them walked far enough, he was bound to question a delivery agency. A receipt showing a parcel delivered from this address, this night. Oh, no.

She even thought of mailing the package to herself at General Delivery. Suppose they watched her? All she had to do was call at the General Delivery window for a package, be stopped, questioned, searched. . . .

She got an old brief case of Lloyd's. She tied up the book and closed it in the brief case. She put on a hat and lightweight coat and left the house. She walked a block, entered a subway kiosk, and rode up to her mother's home.

A block from her mother's apartment she went into a drugstore. She entered a pay booth and called her mother. "Miz Harper," she said, slurring the words, "could you come over to Miz Goldman's already? You haven't heard what is happened?"

"I'll be right over," her mother said. "I'll be right over."

Bernice walked the rest of the way. This was the place where she'd grown up. It was dark. Kids were playing in the street. Grownups lolled on the steps watching the kids. She walked through them, eyes straight ahead. She entered the rear of the apartment house. She used her key, let herself into the apartment. She went into her bedroom. Her mother hadn't changed anything. It was all as Bernice had left it.

In her room there were the same sort of secret places that there were in Bernice's mind. She'd always loved to hide things. She stored them up, the way she stored up

31

resentments and hurts and loneliness. She hid the book. She let herself out of the apartment, returned along the walk as she had come, made perfect subway connections. At nine she re-entered Lloyd's house.

He was yelling for her. He was at the head of the stairs when she came in the front door. "Where did you go?" he demanded.

"I went out," she told him, as women have been telling men who ask too many questions—any questions—since time began.

"What for?"

"I went to get something," she told him. "Now if you'll be good and go back to your room, I'll come up and show you what I have."

She was still carrying the brief case. If someone had seen her leaving with it, she had returned with it. Wasn't she a private secretary? Why shouldn't she carry one?

Lloyd had sent her on an errand. Who was to say he hadn't, after tonight? And when her mother got to Mrs. Goldman's? And no one had called? Mrs. Goldman would be chattering to her mother by now. Neither of them would even think to mention a telephone call. Bernice knew that.

"I'm going out!" Lloyd shouted down at her. "You knew that. Yet you went out. You were gone almost an hour!"

Bernice didn't even answer that. "I'll help you get ready," she said. "I promise you won't be late."

He went back to his room then, still muttering. Bernice turned on the light in the downstairs foyer. Lloyd was going out. That light would be on. Now there was a light in the study, one in the foyer, and one in Lloyd's bedroom upstairs. That was exactly as she wanted it.

She went into the small lavatory beside the study. She got a glass from the medicine chest in there. She unlocked her desk and brought out the fifth of whisky. And now her heart was thudding. Her eyes were bright behind her thick glasses. She started upstairs. The look was in her eyes that she was going to find when she looked in the lavatory mirror later. A look that no one must ever see. A look of exaltation.

Bernice ticked off in her mind the things she had to do, and everything was in place.

"What have you got?" Lloyd said when she entered his bedroom. He was dressed except for his suit coat. His hair was carefully brushed. He had shaved closely.

"I've got something for you to drink," she told him. "You've been good. I want you to have a drink before you go out."

"Let's both have a lot of drinks and I won't go out," he said.

"I'll drink with you," Bernice said. "But you may as well go out. I'll be here when you get back."

His head went up at that. There was something pathetic about him.

"You mean that, Bernice?"

"I'll be here," she said.

He laughed. "Where is the bottle?" She got a glass for him, poured him a drink. She poured one for herself into the glass from the downstairs lavatory.

He drank it down and exhaled pleasurably, making a round O of his mouth. "Good. There isn't another drink in that thing, is there?"

She poured another.

He drank it, and sank down on his bed. "You're good to me, Bernice, all of a sudden. Why?"

"Maybe you were right," she suggested. "Maybe I had to get to know you to get to like you."

He seemed afraid to ask for another drink. A refusal would hurt just at that moment. "Hold your glass," she said, and poured him a double one.

An hour later, Bernice left him singing on the bed. She went downstairs to the study, crossed it, and entered the lavatory. She filled the glass with water, rinsed it well, and replaced it in the medicine chest.

As she came out into the library, the telephone rang.

She ran to her desk and snatched up the receiver before it could shrill again. Suppose Lloyd struggled up enough to answer that telephone in his condition?

"Hello," she said.

It was a man. He was an importer, he said, and gave his name. It sounded like Aboulschetti. "I'd like to speak with Mr. Deerman," he said.

"I'm sorry," she said. Her voice was firm. "This is Mr.

Deerman's secretary. Mr. Deerman is just this minute getting ready to leave the house. If you'd care to call in the morning—"

"But—"

"In the morning," Bernice said. She replaced the receiver.

On the way upstairs she did something she hadn't done for a long time. She prayed.

Not for herself. And not for the soul of Lloyd Deerman. But just that the telephone wouldn't ring while she was this far from it.

The thought sent her running upstairs and into Lloyd's bedroom. She found him sprawled out on his back across the bed.

"Get up," she said. "Get your coat on. It's time to go."

Lloyd struggled up on his elbows. His head flopped forward.

"Go? Are you kiddin', Bernice? I couldn't go anywhere like this."

"You're all right. Let me help you with your coat." Oh, wonderful, she thought, I've overdone it. In a night club he consumes a bottle of Scotch. Tonight, with half a dozen drinks, he's limp as a dishcloth. "What will your friends think?"

"Who cares? Nobody. Goin' to see a man 'bout some dog-eared rugs. Name's Abulchetty. Something. Called this morning. 'Member? Or did I tell you? Arab. Arab stuff. Don't give God Almighty 'bout it—"

Bernice felt cold between her shoulder blades. Abulchetty had just called. Suppose he had called to cancel the appointment? She decided she had to force it, before the rug importer called back.

"He just called," she said. "Do you hear? You're late now. Lloyd, get up. If you don't get a grip on yourself, I—well, whatever I said, I—I couldn't mean it."

"I didn't believe you meant it, anyway," he snarled at her. But he stood up and shrugged into his coat. She helped him across the room.

Her breathing was ragged now. Lloyd staggered out into the hall. She stared at the steep old stairwell. Her mouth parted. This was it. No rehearsal. No second chances. No misses allowed. It had to be quick, vicious, and right. She had no idea how hard a man could fall without dying, or how long it would take him to die. She knew only that Lloyd had to fall, and Lloyd had to die.

At the mouth of the stairwell she stepped back from Lloyd. She cried out as though missing her step. Arms outstretched like two thin battering rams, she struck against the tottering giant.

He spun almost all the way around on his heels, bending at the waist. For one horrible second, Bernice thought he was going to fall toward her. With paralytic motion he reached out for her, and then toppled backward. He didn't utter a sound. His head struck the sharp edge of his wall guide rail. It sounded like the crack of a whip. Then he bounced away from the wall and sprawled out helplessly, striking head and shoulders first. His legs rolled over him then. The whole house shook. He landed against the railing. Bernice heard it rip and shatter under his weight. The flooring beneath her quivered. Bernice began to be paralyzed. By the time he had stopped twisting and rolling down the steps and lay sprawled out over the lower stairs, Bernice was rigid. For the moment, she was unable to move.

She stood at the head of the stairs, staring down at him.

He had lost his glasses in the fall. His empty, sightless eyes, white as slugs, were fixed on her at a crazy angle, because his head was twisted over his left shoulder.

Bernice thought sickly that she might have loved him, except for those hideous, sightless eyes. Eyes that had never seen her.

But eyes that were watching her now.

Chapter Four

B ernice was clever.
She told Findlay where she and Lloyd had met, how much he had offered her to leave Brennan's and work for him. She looked at the detective. How could I refuse such an offer? her glance inquired. He made another note in his little black book. She explained again that she had been

transcribing a letter. The paper was still in the typewriter. She gestured toward it. Lloyd had called out to her from upstairs. He was going out and was impatient when she didn't answer quickly enough. When she came out into the lower foyer, Lloyd was already at the head of the stairs. She cried out, warning him. Then like something in a nightmare, she saw him trip, sprawl out, and fall down the stairs. She didn't know until she smelled his breath that he was drunk. She had no idea where he had got the whisky, or how he had smuggled it into the house. Findlay nodded gravely. Her score: perfect. It was just that Findlay didn't believe her.

Other people came into the library. She felt better. Less alone. Less afraid.

Clive Behrens flopped into an easy chair. The lawyer was a classically handsome man in an expensively tailored suit. He was forty-nine. He'd been closely associated with Lloyd Deerman for the past fifteen years. He had known Lloyd in Deerman's better years. Behrens continued to overlook the impatience and bitterness growing in Lloyd. He still considered Lloyd a rather heroic figure. A man who'd overcome terrific odds. Built up a fortune.

Joe Sanders was Lloyd's business partner. He was a thin, salmon-colored man. He must have been in bed somewhere when his wife had located him. He was hastily dressed. When he sat in a leather chair and pinked up his trousers at the knees, you could see he hadn't taken time to put on his socks.

Marsha Deerman was a stout little woman with graying hair. Her face was splotched from her weeping. She sat in a straight chair, her shoulders round. Her daughter, Francie, was a lovely brunette girl. She appeared slightly startled at the facts of life—or perhaps it was the way she plucked her eyebrows. But she was exceptionally pretty. In a few years she was going to be darkly beautiful.

Francie pulled a straight chair over and sat close to her mother. She patted her stout hand as they waited. Dr. Mundy sat alone on the leather divan, reclining at one end with his arm resting on its side.

Findlay spoke first to Marsha Deerman. "I'm very sorry about what has happened to your son, Mrs. Deerman.

Anything I say, it's just that I'm doing my job. I hope you'll understand that. I'm only making sure that your son's death was accidental."

Marsha interrupted him. She looked up, her eyes red-rimmed. "I'm sure it was an accident," she said huskily.

"Oh?" Findlay looked at her. "Are you?"

"Of course. Why must you—why must you make something else of it? My poor son fell down the stairs. In my fears it has happened a hundred times before. I didn't want him to live here alone."

"Doesn't that seem rather pat?" Findlay inquired. "He was going to fall down the stairs. Everybody knew it. Now tonight he has done it."

"He had been drinking," Mrs. Deerman whispered.

Findlay nodded. "Yes."

"He was often drunk," she persisted. "He was my son, Mr. Findlay. I knew his strength. And—I knew his weakness. I'm sure Dr. Mundy will tell you it was—an accident."

"I already have stated that," Mundy said.

Findlay looked at him a moment. Then the detective's eyes moved across Bernice and back to Marsha Deerman.

"How well do you know Miss Harper?" he said.

"I've known her during these last few months. My son spoke very warmly of her."

"Oh? He did?"

"Very highly of her."

Findlay nodded. "Thank you, Mrs. Deerman," he said.

Mundy broke in. "I'm sure you're doing your job, Findlay," he said. "But I was talking with the medical examiner—"

"I'll talk to him, too," Findlay said. "Just a few questions. If you don't mind, Doctor. I'm representing the police department here tonight. Long as I do, I'll have to do it my way."

"What's clearly an accident need not be subjected to scrutiny by the homicide bureau," Mundy said.

"All right," Findlay said. There was an edge to his gray voice. "Let's say I'll be brief about this, then." He faced the lawyer.

"Mr. Behrens, I know it will be some time before Mr. Deerman's will can be probated and read. I want to know only one thing about that will. Has it been changed—" he consulted his notebook—"within the last six months?"

Behrens smiled at him. "Deerman wasn't a man to change his mind and his will precipitately. I assure you that his will was not altered in the last four years."

Findlay shrugged, wrote in his notebook, and thanked the lawyer.

Bernice sat behind her desk. From beneath the glinting barrier of her glasses, she watched the people as Findlay questioned them.

Sanders was next.

Sanders said, "No, Mr. Findlay. The account books would have to be audited. But so far as I know, and our firm isn't so large that I'm out of touch with the bookkeeping department, Mr. Deerman hasn't withdrawn anything but his expense allowances in the past year."

"And if anything like that happened, you would be told about it?"

"I certainly would." Sanders laughed. "Besides, Lloyd and I were close. We had no secrets from each other."

Bernice felt laughter stirring in her throat. She was thinking about the false-fronted account book, hidden in her room in her mother's Bronx apartment. No secrets?

"All right," Findlay said. He turned to Bernice. "When you saw that Deerman was dead, why didn't you call the police?"

"I didn't know he was dead."

"She called me," Mundy interposed. "Immediately."

"Why didn't you call an ambulance?"

"I didn't know what to do. I was frightened. I knew Dr. Mundy. The first thing I thought was to call him."

"A very smart first thought, Miss Harper. Let a doctor pronounce him dead. You notice the lights that are burning, the whisky on Deerman's breath, the fact that the servants are out of the house, and the first thing you think of is to call the doctor. Or were you simply too smart to call the police?"

Behrens said, "Just a minute, Findlay. That's pretty rugged."

Joe Sanders said, "What's smart about calling the police?"

"It's a good idea," Findlay replied. "Alone in the house. A fall."

"I think I'd have done what Bernice did," Sanders said. "I'd have called the doctor. He lives near. He would know what to do."

"Shall we score another point for Miss Harper?" Findlay said. His gaze moved over them. "Let's look at it this way. Deerman was drunk. How many times have you seen a drunk that's been run over by a speeding car get up and walk away? Why, a drunk could fall off a church steeple and not get hurt."

"Which makes the case for accidental death that much stronger," Behrens said. "It was an impossible thing. You're suggesting that Bernice Harper is a very sinister and clever woman. If she were as clever as you suggest, she'd know that there was not a chance in the world that a man as big as Lloyd would be killed falling down stairs even as steep as those."

"Perhaps that explains the place where Deerman was hit at the back of his head?" Findlay said.

"No," said Mundy. "The loose inside guide rail explains that. He reached for the newel post, tripped, spun around, cracked his head on the guide rail, and loosened it from the wall plaster."

"Yes," Findlay said. "That could be the explanation. Or it could be an explanation. Did he strike—or was he struck?"

Behrens snorted. "Will you get your salary this month, Findlay, without making a murder of my client's death? Or are you paid on commission?"

Findlay looked at him. "You know how we are paid," he said. "And how little."

"Then why don't you relax?" Behrens said. "Such devotion to duty is just a little chilling."

Findlay didn't answer Behrens. He looked at Bernice. Her face remained set. Her mouth was a straight line.

"You have a good score, Miss Harper. All your answers check and double check. Everybody is sure you're innocent. I never saw a better score. A girl making a good salary, pleased with her job. No changed will, no insurance benefits. I'll go out now and talk with the medical examiner.

None of you folks need stay, I guess. Maybe you would like to go up to your mother's for tonight, Miss Harper? I'll get a cab for you, if you like. Would you like that? It's not that I bear you malice. How could I? We never met before. If you're lucky, you'll never see me again. I have a feeling you're going to be lucky. I have a feeling there won't even be an inquest. I'm pretty sure the M. E.'s office will release Mr. Deerman's body to any funeral parlor his mother would care to select. How about that, Mrs. Deerman? Of course, I'm not the final word on that. But it's just a feeling I have. So if you'll excuse me, I'll go out and talk to the M. E."

Bernice felt the breath sigh across her lips.

When she exhaled, her lungs burned and ached. She had no idea how long she'd been holding her breath.

Chapter Five

"That awful detective!" Marsha Deerman said.

She was holding both of Bernice's hands. She was dressed in black. She had been wearing mourning the week since Lloyd's death. She would continue to wear it. Lloyd had been her whole world. She had blamed herself that he was blind. He made a fortune alone and it seemed to her that he'd done it in part for her. Lloyd had been trying to show her he didn't hate her because he was blind. When he drank, she understood. She could feel all his bitterness and loneliness. And when he died, part of her died with him.

"I wanted to hit that Findlay," Francie said. "I wanted somebody to hit him."

"He was doing his job," Bernice said. No one would notice that she was bearing black. The dress did nothing for her. Francie's showed off her figure. Mrs. Deerman's displayed the darkness of her grief. "After all, I was the only person in the house. He had to suspect somebody."

"Why?" Mrs. Deerman said. "Even the medical examiner said it was just one of those freak accidents that simply happen. I think my son had fallen before. He would never admit it. But once when I visited him, he was very bruised

40

and couldn't get around at all well. He only laughed at me when I questioned him, but I was sure that he had fallen."

My God, Bernice thought, suppose he hadn't died. Suppose he had lived, knowing that I had pushed him. She shivered.

"There," Mrs. Deerman said. "The police have closed the whole case. It was an accident. We won't talk about it."

"Just the same," Francie said, "I never saw a man I hated more than I did that detective."

"I was afraid of him," Bernice admitted.

"Weren't you, though?" Francie said. "I just got the creeps watching him."

"It's time to go," Mrs. Deerman said. "I want to tell you, Bernice, how much Francie and I appreciate your coming along with us to Mr. Behren's office. We're so helpless. Both of us. We can't thank you enough for standing by us like this."

"It's the least I can do," Bernice said.

It was the last thing she wanted to do. She never wanted to see any of the Deermans again. She wanted to get Lloyd out of her mind.

Earlier in the week she had gone to her mother's apartment and removed the money from Lloyd's account book. On her next visit to Deerman's old house she had replaced the empty account book on its shelf.

She thought, Wouldn't Findlay love to poke around and find that book? What if he did? And what if it was empty? There was nothing to show it had ever held almost twenty-five thousand dollars in tight green stacks. There was no title pasted on it as there was on each of the others. And if her fingerprints were all over it? So were they all over the other account books, too.

Let him find it, she thought coldly. Seven days had passed. She'd not seen him again. She forgot the cold thread of fear that stitched a tight patch at the base of her throat when his gray eyes settled on her.

She thought impatiently, I want to get away. Away from Lloyd's mother and Lloyd's sister, and Findlay, and everything that reminds me of Lloyd. I'll be all right then. . . .

"I want you to know you won't be forgotten," Mrs. Deerman was saying. Bernice had to drag her attention back to the stout woman. "Lloyd spoke warmly of you. He wouldn't have forgotten you if his accident hadn't taken him so—so untimely. We'll see you're not forgotten, Bernice."

Bernice flushed, wishing she could get away from the woman's kindness. "I don't expect anything," she said.

"Of course you don't, dear. But it would be Lloyd's wish."

"Mother has spoken to Joe Sanders about it," Francie said.

The first person Bernice saw in Behrens' plush office was Fred Findlay.

He was a gray shadow in a corner of the fifteenth-story office. Anger beat inside Bernice. He's hounding me. I won't have it. I won't. I won't.

She felt her throat tighten up. Findlay seemed unaware of her. The room was crowded with other people. Lloyd's three servants were there. They nodded briefly at Bernice.

It was not that they disliked her or suspected her. They each one found her without charm. That was all. Bernice thought, They laughed when I sat down at my typewriter. They felt Lloyd should have had a movie queen to take his dictation. Poor, plain little Bernice. That had been in their faces. Well, she hadn't liked them, either.

Behrens said, "We all know why we are here. The people here are business associates, servants, or relatives of my late client and pal, Lloyd Deerman. It wouldn't be feasible to attempt to introduce you people to each other. So to get into the thing, I'm going to tell you that I'm Clive Behrens, attorney at law, and that I'm going to read the provisions of Mr. Deerman's last will and testament."

To Bernice, the will was involved and detailed. One fact made an impression on her as Behrens read. Lloyd Deerman had been a very wealthy man. She sat there, feeling Findlay's gray eyes fixed on a spot at the nape of her neck. She knew she could have married Lloyd Deerman and had all that wealth.

She shrugged her coat up about her neck. She didn't regret what she had done. Not all his money would have made it worth being his seeing-eye wife. No. She would buy what she wanted, with the money she had got from him.

Each of the servants received a thousand dollars each. All the relatives were remembered, and all his business associates who had been with him longer than five years.

Finally it was over. The relatives straggled out of the office. Behrens motioned for Bernice to remain in her chair. It seemed that suddenly there were only three people remaining in Behrens' office: Bernice, Behrens, and Fred Findlay.

Bernice tightened her fingers on her purse to keep them from trembling. She wanted to run. She was sure something had gone wrong. Findlay had kept poking around. She had made one mistake, she couldn't even think what, and Findlay had found it.

She held herself rigid in her chair. Findlay sat down beside her.

"Hello, Miss Harper."

"Hello, Mr. Findlay."

"I did you an injustice last week," Findlay said.

Bernice felt her heart slow a little. "Did you?"

"Don't you want to know what I mean?"

"No. You found me innocent. I knew that all the time."

"I had my job to do," he said. "The department has closed the case. It was an accident. I only came to hear the will. You're mentioned nowhere. There's no insurance tie-up. You're in the clear. I just wanted to tell you, you're looking better. I've seen it happen. A woman has her first baby and blossoms out into a real beauty. Or she paints a masterpiece. Or flies an ocean, or writes a book—and she's no longer the same. She doesn't even look the same any more. Changes 'em. Some kind of inner chemistry, I guess. Havin' a baby, writin' a book, paintin' a picture—"

"Or killing a man." Bernice's voice was loud.

Behrens' head jerked up. "Not in here, Findlay!" he snapped. "You told me you wanted to hear the will read. I agreed to let you. Lloyd's death has been officially called an accident. I didn't allow you in here so you could hound Miss Harper."

"I didn't mean to," Findlay demurred. "I was trying to pay her a compliment."

Bernice stared at him. She knew her face was flushed.

43

She could feel her cheeks burn. "I didn't like it," she said. She had to force her voice to remain level.

Findlay said he was sorry. But Bernice was looking at him. His face didn't change, he didn't look sorry. He didn't seem to be laughing, either. But Bernice knew he was.

Inside, Findlay was roaring with laughter. Pleased as hell.

Behrens came around his desk. Something about him, the way he walked, the way he held his wide shoulders, excited Bernice. She wondered what it would be like to go to bed with him. My God, she thought, it's been years since I thought a thing like that about any man. He was old enough to be her father. And she knew that didn't matter, either. . . .

She was more aware of the chemical fusions and stirrings in the crannies of her body than she was of what he was saying. She had to force herself to listen to the meaning of his words and not the hypnotic timbre of his deep voice.

He sat on a chair beside her and crossed his knees. She was aware that he was holding out a business card to her.

"Joe Sanders asked me to give this to you," Behrens said. "He said you could have an appointment with him at your convenience today at this address. I hope you'll go this morning, Miss Harper."

Joseph Sanders kept her waiting an hour.

Just when Bernice had made up her mind to tell Sanders' full-breasted secretary that she would come back later, he sent word for her to come into his private office.

"Sorry, but the things that came up were urgent," Sanders said when she sat beside his desk. He had spread his lunch out on his blotter—milk and soda crackers. Sanders suffered from ulcers. "I'd ask you to join me," he said with a smile, "but I don't even like the stuff."

If she'd been lovely enough, she thought, he'd have taken her to lunch instead of asking her in here to see him eat crackers soaked in milk.

"We wanted to do something for you, Bernice," Sanders said. "The whole family—and the firm. Lloyd would have wanted us to."

"I don't expect anything," Bernice said.

He glanced at her, his expression saying, Naturally you

don't. You should have been happy as hell with Lloyd.

"If there were any openings with the firm . . ." Sanders said. But the regret in his voice wasn't well done. Bernice looked at him. She let him see that she knew he was lying. "Just now there isn't a thing. Why, I wouldn't ask you to take what I could offer just now. I'm sure, though, you'll get on somewhere without any trouble."

"I'm sure I will."

"I know you will. Because I'm going to give you references that will get you in anywhere, Bernice."

Except here, she thought.

He handed her a thick envelope with a Deerman & Sanders return address. She took it and thanked him without warmth. She stuffed it into her handbag.

"Well, and that's just part of it, Bernice. We all got together. Marsha Deerman, Behrens, all of us. We want to make you a gift. Naturally, you weren't mentioned in Lloyd's will. But he regarded you highly"—his unbelieving eyes went over her again—"and though he died without making any provision for you, you're not forgotten. Lloyd and I were close. No secrets between us. That's why we've been so successful. They left the actual gift up to me, and Bernice, I want you to know that when I give you this five hundred dollars, it comes from all our hearts."

Five hundred dollars. Five hundred. Five. Five hundred dollars. His servants got twice that. You're looking at me, thinking Lloyd took me to bed with him, pitying him because he was blind, and thinking he had no taste, but sure I was his mistress. And you're making me a gift from your heart. Five hundred dollars.

She longed to laugh at him. She wanted to laugh in his face. She could even feel the laughter swirling and itching in her throat. Oh, but it didn't matter. The money didn't matter. The insulting little man with his ulcers and his milk and crackers, he didn't matter either.

But to have to take that five hundred dollars!

To have to thank him for it.

Bernice felt her face twist into a false, ugly smile. So false it made her teeth itch.

But she took the money. And she managed to thank him.

Chapter Six

Bernice ran toward the plaster bridge.

The inverted mushrooms, pink, green, and gaudy orange, quivered and undulated as she sped past.

The color of the water didn't frighten Bernice any more. Nothing mattered except that she must cross the white plaster bridge that spanned the odd-shaped pool. She had to get to the other side, where there was laughter. Where Bernice looked lovelier even than Rita Baehrs. More beautiful than Rita, who could trade beauty for advancement! The thought made Bernice run faster. It made her close her eyes to the awful bloody color of the stagnant water.

She began to feel free. Self-confidence flowed into her and her step was steadier. For the first time she knew where she was going—across that bridge and upward along the hillside to the sunlit crest.

Behind her Bernice could hear the rumbling of subway trains, the cry of somebody's whistling teakettle. She remembered how popular they'd been up in the Bronx. Everybody was buying them at Woolworth's. The teakettles, the subway, the shouting trailed after her. But she didn't care, because she knew it could never touch her now.

The smells belonged to a kitchen. Meat loaf, strong with onions. Roast beef. Boiled foods. But even the odors were weaker, the nearer she came to the little bridge.

She didn't even hesitate at the brink of the pool. She stretched out her foot, feeling the warm breeze that was coming down the pleasant hill into the gaudy room of mushrooms.

But as her foot touched the plaster bridge, it shattered under her feet.

The sound of its ripping and tearing was exactly the sound the stair railings had made the night Lloyd's huge body toppled crazily against them as he plunged down the steep stairs to his death.

In horror and panic, Bernice thought, I'll fall into the pool! I'll fall into the blood-colored water!

She tried to leap back from the shattering bridge, but she couldn't. She'd been running too fast, the bridge was too flimsy.

She sprawled out, arms flung ahead of her. The pool was so small. Maybe she'd fall beyond it.

She was thrown downward, headfirst. But she didn't land in the water, nor did she strike the other side of the pool.

She began to fall, rolling and twisting down into nothingness. She had a horrible sense of loneliness. Loneliness more than the fear of being injured. She was without support, without security, she was falling and there was no one to help her. The fall snatched her breath away. She reached out in terror, seeking something to cling to. She began to scream.

She woke up, wet with sweat. She had the giddy sense of having screamed as she woke up. For a long time she lay in the darkness, panting. She couldn't have screamed. Someone would have heard her.

Her breathing slowed. She rolled over on her side. The covers were twisted under her. Her window was opened to the night. The sounds of the city, subways, moving vans, the sudden starting of cars, the noises that never cease, floated up into her room.

For a moment Bernice couldn't even remember where she was.

The familiar objects of her apartment took shape in the darkness. It was a month now since Lloyd had died. Bernice assured herself she never thought of it any other way. She had rented these rooms. She wanted to be alone. She wanted to escape the baleful glances of her mother. She wanted to begin the wonderful new life she dreamed for herself.

She swung her feet off the bed. She went over to her window, feeling a moment of giddiness as she stood beside it. She wondered how it would feel to lift her legs over the sill and walk out there into emptiness, walk and fall, the way she did in her dreams.

She watched the stragglers move along the street below her. Their shadows bobbed at their sides. Even those people seemed to have somewhere to go.

She pressed her fingers against her aching forehead. She knew she needed to get out of this room. She needed to be among people, people who knew how to laugh and enjoy themselves. That was the only way she was going to get Lloyd out of her mind. Alone in this room, she had only to close her eyes. She could see Lloyd then, lying at the foot of the wide stairs, neck twisted back, sightless eyes watching her.

Her breath quickened. I'll get over that, too, she told herself. She was willing to pay for what she wanted—and that was part of the payment. But she had a new fear now.

Hadn't it been too easy?

Everyone but the detective Fred Findlay had believed her. Lloyd Deerman was forgotten by almost everyone as though he had never even existed. It had been too easy.

She turned on the lights and got the twenty-odd thousand dollars from its hiding place. Smiling a little, she slowly counted it.

The green bills leered and winked up at her. It was almost as if they dared her to begin spending them.

Dared her. Her breath caught. Her fingers clenched on the money.

Perhaps, she thought, the money is counterfeit!

Why not? Was that too fantastic? Why had Lloyd hidden it so carelessly in his study? At first it had seemed a good hiding place. Who would think of his dusty account books as a cache? But now the idea seemed preposterous. As a matter of fact, where had the money come from? Wasn't Lloyd an importer? Wasn't he a blind importer as well? Maybe he had got mixed in some secret deal with someone like Abulchetty—or some other silly name—and been paid off in lovely counterfeit dollars. He couldn't yell copper if the deal were shady, could he? What could he do?

She was suddenly violently ill at her stomach. He could have done—just what he did. Put that money in a book in his study. A constant reminder against shady deals involving—oh, my good God in heaven, Bernice sobbed inside—counterfeit money!

48

She stared at the open window with its curtains barely stirring in the early-morning breezes. Her teeth began to chatter. She pushed the money away from her and it fell in stacks about her feet. Voices screamed at her from bottom-less voids, empty, frightening voices, crying and weeping at her. Die, Bernice, die. Get out of it. Run away from it. Escape, Bernice. Die!

She clenched her teeth together to keep them from shaking. Her thin fists were knotted in her lap. She looked down at the lovely nightgown she'd bought. That was only to be the beginning. She looked about the room. All the time those wailing voices sobbed inside her. I'll kill myself if this money isn't real. I won't live, I won't go on living.

She got up. She stepped on the money as she prowled the room. It wasn't the first time those voices had sobbed inside her mind. They were often there. They'd been there many times before. When hurts and bitterness piled up, and there seemed to be no use to try to go on living, she'd heard those whispering voices. They begged her to die. But they'd never been so real or so violent as they were at this moment.

Nothing has ever been so important before.

She tried to stay away from that window as she paced the room. But she was drawn to it. And when finally she did walk almost to it, some unbearable weight dragged at her, pulling her across the open sill. She sank to her knees and the weight settled at the nape of her neck. She laid her head against the window facing.

She was afraid to spend the money now. Yet she knew she had to try. She had killed for it, for what she wanted. She didn't know how she would wait through the rest of the night, but when morning came, she would try to spend the money.

She sobbed tiredly. She had to try. She had to know.

Bernice dressed carefully. She brushed her hair, thinking of a vain general going to his execution. He would die looking his best, with his boots polished. It was like that with Bernice. She hadn't dared buy clothes and accessories yet. But she was wearing the best she owned. At least she'd look her best when she found out that she had killed for nothing; for less than nothing—for counterfeit money.

She had hidden the money again. For a moment she surveyed the room. She went along the hall and down the elevator to the street.

The brilliance of the morning sun hurt Bernice's eyes. Her head began to ache. But Bernice hardly noticed the pain. It wasn't important enough to matter now.

She looked at the crowds at the bus stop, chattering dialects from the various corners of New York City. She hesitated before a gleaming cafeteria. But she knew she couldn't even keep a cup of coffee on her stomach this morning. She kept walking.

In her purse was a single hundred-dollar bill. It was from the stacks of money she had removed from Lloyd's study. There was nothing else in her purse. Not even personal identification.

If the money were worthless, Bernice had no further plans.

The Citizen's Bank. Bernice hesitated before the narrow smoke-blackened façade of the building. She could feel the stirring of those voices in her mind. She longed to turn and run.

She pushed through the front door.

A guard nodded to her. He was wearing an olive-drab uniform. A small pistol was holstered at his hip.

"The tellers?" she said to him. She sounded like a crow, she thought miserably.

"Those wickets to your left, miss," the guard said.

Her legs weighted and tired, Bernice started across the polished flooring. She unclasped the top of her purse, shoved her hand inside. Her fingers closed on the money.

She was at the barred window. She brought the money up in her fist. Her heart beat erratically, slowed, and seemed to stop. She forced her hand to move casually and she thrust the bill through the window.

"Change, please," she said. She was surprised. Her voice was calm.

Her eyes met the green ones of the teller. He smiled, a deep, white-toothed grin in a blond, handsome face. Handsome. As a Greek god. As a movie star. Like the fulfillment of her fondest dream. She let her gaze fall to the plate where his name was neatly lettered: Mr. Carlos Brandon.

She could feel his eyes on her face. She looked up. He had turned the bill over in his lean, tanned hand.

"Just a moment," he said.

My God, Bernice thought, suppose I faint.

Chapter Seven

Two minutes can seem like an hour. That's what it seemed to Bernice, awaiting change for her hundred-dollar bill, She stood there, feeling the perspiration standing in separate chilled globules across her forehead, wondering if her knees were going to support her.

She watched the extraordinarily handsome teller, Carlos Brandon. He slid the green note into his drawer and riffled through some smaller bills.

She wanted to laugh aloud. She wanted to cry in the abrupt relief she felt. The money is good. It's all right. I can spend it. I can go on living. I can begin to live.

The teller looked up. He was smiling at her. "How would you like your change, miss?" he said.

"Oh, I don't mind. Any way at all."

He counted it out in tens, fives, and ones. He pushed them through the opening.

She covered the money with her icy fingers. It didn't seem possible that just a few minutes ago her very life had depended on whether or not that hundred-dollar bill was counterfeit. Now it wasn't important any more at all. There were all those other lovely bills. She could spend them, buying the things she'd wanted for twenty-four years.

She could look at the teller and know that he was what she had dreamed of in those excited nights. That he was what she wanted now. He was what a beautiful girl would have—a handsome man. When she walked with him, people would turn to stare across their shoulders. But better than that, he would excite her and he would thrill her, and he would make her gentle, and he would drive her wild.

She smiled as the vagary flitted through her mind. He was a teller in a bank, probably married, probably had two

51

kids and plenty of debts. And even if he wasn't, how could she ever meet him? She pushed the money into her empty purse, aware that she was still smiling.

Aware that her hungry longing was probably naked in her eyes!

"Work around here?" he said.

There was no one waiting behind her. She looked at him, feeling that old fright, that old anxiety. She forced herself to conceal her panic behind her smile. "Yes," she lied. "Just down the street."

"Nice," Carlos Brandon said. "Maybe I'll see you again. Sometime. When you get another one of those things you want changed."

She felt the warmth stirring inside her, seeping over the doubt that assailed her. How could a handsome man like Brandon be interested in her? But he was interested. He was looking her over guardedly.

"That may be sooner than you think," she said.

"I'll be looking for you. Remember, don't trade anywhere else."

"Oh, no," she said. "I wouldn't think of it."

She snapped her purse, turning a little. He leaned forward. She felt her heart thudding. She knew she should move on. But for the moment, she couldn't.

"Swell day out, isn't it?" he said. "Too bad I'm tied in here until four."

You're it, baby, his green eyes were whispering. You're it for me, and you know it. Whether it's in a bank or in a park or in a zoo, or at a party somewhere, this is it.

Panic made her voice shaky. "Four?" she said. Her voice rose a little. "Four o'clock? Isn't that odd? That's the time I'm off from work today."

He looked at her. "Maybe I'll see you," he said. His voice was telling her that he would see her. He would tell her where to be. And she would be there. How wonderful, Bernice thought. Nothing like this could ever happen to me at Brennans. There was no one like Carlos Brandon in that whole establishment. But wouldn't she love to have Rita Baehrs see her with Carlos?

She nodded, breathless. "If you want to."

"Sure I want to." There were three impatient people behind Bernice now. He was unaware of them. "It's lonely in a big town. How about it, isn't it lonely for you?"

"Oh, I have my friends. I've always lived here. But I couldn't let a stranger in town be lonely. Could I? I'll have coffee in the café at the corner. This afternoon. When—I get off work."

"At four? That'll be wonderful."

She was at a small booth in the crowded little corner café at four o'clock. She saw Carlos come down the two steps and stand for a moment in the entrance. She waited, wondering if he would recognize her, coldly afraid that he wouldn't.

His eyes trailed across her, moved back, smiling. Bernice's heart flopped over. She would have sworn it did.

He came through the crowded aisle. He was tall, six feet tall, anyway. You couldn't find a blemish in his perfection. Maybe, just maybe, he looked a little harried about the eyes.

He sat in the booth across from her. He ordered coffee for himself and smiled again. It was an intimate, personal smile that looked rehearsed as hell. Even Bernice felt that. But she couldn't think of any reason why he should try a professional approach.

He dropped four lumps of sugar in his coffee and leaned across the table. "What's your name? By the way, I'm—"

"Carlos Brandon," she said.

"Oh. Been reading my name plate at the bank. You know, I wondered if people ever looked at that thing."

"It's a beautiful name," Bernice said. "Isn't Carlos kind of Spanish?"

"Spanish as Mulligan stew," he told her with a grin. "My mother read a book once. She thought it was a romantic name. Still, it could have been worse. She could have named me Farmall, after one of my old man's tractors."

"Oh, did you come from a farm?"

"Right. Just as fast as I could. That four A.M. stuff is for the birds. That's the time of day I like to go to bed."

Bernice laughed appreciatively. As a matter of fact, she appreciated it. This restaurant on a shabby avenue was transformed for her; all the people looked young and

53

happy. Carlos was watching her, his hazel eyes smiling over his coffee cup. He was not only the most handsome man she had ever seen, he was the first one who had ever seemed genuinely interested in her. There were twenty-four years of hunger behind this delicious moment of triumph for Bernice. She felt giddy. She wanted to laugh out loud. She wondered how she could delay the moment of their parting. She was already dreading the time when he would leave her.

"My name is Bernice," she said. "Bernice Harper. I haven't any interesting past. I'm not running away from anything like you are."

His eyes flickered. He set the cup down heavily, frowning. "Like I am?"

"I mean from the farm. I was born in the Bronx. I guess, though everybody runs away from the Bronx. Maybe that's what I'm doing."

"Maybe we can run away together," he said lightly. But looking at him, Bernice saw his mouth go bitter, and she knew his thoughts were fixed on some hell inside himself. Now he laughed briefly. "I'm not where I want to be yet. Are you, Bernice?"

He was smiling. But his eyes were watching her face, strangely, intently. She met his gaze. "No," she said. "No, I'm not."

They came out into the sunlight of late afternoon and stood for a moment before the white front of the café. Bernice felt a thrust of panic. He was going to leave her. He'd said nothing about seeing her again. Why should he? She felt tongue-tied and awkward and unlovely beside him. And besides, she told herself she was a fool to try to cling to the first man she saw that she wanted. Maybe a girl had to learn how to interest a man. But, she thought angrily, no matter what I see from this moment, it will still be Carlos Brandon that I want, that I think about.

She looked up at him, hoping the bleakness she felt wasn't showing in her face.

He smiled. "What shall we do, Bernice? Ride a bus? Go to Grant's Tomb? I'm sorry. I can't ask you anywhere decent, Bernice. I—well, damn it, I may as well be honest. I like you. And you see somebody you like, you ought to be honest with them, shouldn't you?"

"Oh, yes," Bernice breathed.

"See, it's this way. I haven't been at the bank very long. I've had to send money home. Well, right now, I'm just at a place where a guy hasn't the right to ask a girl even to have coffee with him."

"Why, that's all right," Bernice said. "Goodness. I understand. Besides, I have money. You saw me change it. I haven't spent a penny of it."

"That's out," he said. He even looked a little offended.

"Oh, I'm sorry!" Bernice cried. "I didn't mean to hurt your feelings. I was thinking about it as a loan. But anyway, you don't have to take me any special place. Why, we can go up to my apartment. I'd cook supper for us. How would you like that?"

"Home cooking?" Carlos said. "It sounds swell."

On the way to Bernice's apartment, Carlos bought a small bottle of grocery-store wine.

He sat in the front room while she changed her dress. She rejoined him, wearing a simple house frock. Carlos had poured them a drink of wine.

She sat beside him on the couch. They toasted each other and drank. Bernice began to feel the effects of it at once. She hadn't eaten all day. The relief and awe at finding she was wealthy, and the excitement of meeting Carlos and having him alone in the same room with her, set her mind to whirling. The wine did the rest.

She laughed. It had an odd ring. Carlos looked at her. He frowned.

"Now wait, Bernice," he laughed. "You gonna get looped on one little glass of wine?"

"I'm not used to wine," she said. "I'm not used to men. Like you. I'm just excited. Don't mind me."

Her face was damp and flushed. She moistened her lips with the tip of her tongue. She leaned toward him. My God, Bernice, she thought, wait at least until he pushes you over!

"Don't be afraid," she whispered. "I could take off my glasses if you like."

"I'm not afraid of your glasses."

"Are you afraid of me? Are you afraid I'll eat you up? You better be. I might."

That was animal, she thought. Pure animal. She saw that Carlos knew it too. And he was stirred. She wavered toward him.

"Hey," he said. His voice was at boudoir pitch. "You're liable to get yourself all tangled up if you go around talking like that. We better go start supper."

Bernice stared at him. She sank against the couch. Her slugging heart made her breathing labored. Her chilled fingers were trembling.

"All right," she said.

Carlos left right after dinner. He helped her do the dishes. He spent the whole time talking about her. Questions. Where she had worked, whom she'd known, where she'd lived. Even disappointed as she was, Bernice couldn't tell herself that she was rejected. It was just that he began to watch the clock about seven. He became nervous and abstracted.

Bernice trailed into the front room, flopped on the couch. Probably he's married, she told herself bitterly. Something has to be wrong, doesn't it? Why would a handsome man like Carlos look twice at her? Probably he was hurrying home to wife, kids, and second mortgage. But she didn't believe that. If he had been married, he wouldn't have passed up that opportunity on the couch before dinner. That's what he would have been looking for, wouldn't it? And he had pointedly avoided it.

She lay there. She tried to imagine what might have happened if he had taken her in his arms.

She got up from the couch and wandered around the room. She stood at her window. Couples walked together on the sidewalks below, or stood close together in the dark places. They had so much to say to each other. She watched a man hunched close over a girl in a doorway. It was as though the girl were cold and they both knew it, and both of them knew the girl needed the man's body close to warm her.

Bernice lay sleepless all night long. She couldn't get the handsome face of Carlos Brandon out of her mind. She tried to tell herself Carlos didn't want her. If he had, he would have taken her on the couch. He would have said something about seeing her again. He hadn't touched her at all.

She twisted, feeling the covers knot under her hips.

But Carlos had seemed interested. What had he said? "Maybe we can run away together, Bernice. I'm not where I want to be yet. Are you?" He'd just been talking. A handsome man on a date. Making conversation. Only, her breath quickened. His eyes had looked worried, and as he spoke his mouth tightened bitterly. Maybe he would like to get away. She had money enough to make that possible. It would be like buying him. But Bernice couldn't think of anything she'd rather spend her money for.

She could feel the perspiration oozing through the pores of her body. Obviously, Carlos Brandon was very poor. There was something nagging at his mind. He was worried. He had been honest when he said he wanted to get away. If she were willing to pay all expenses— She'd be subtle about it. Why wouldn't Carlos be glad to go away with her?

She shook her head. She didn't even know when she would see him again. He had told her nothing about himself. He hadn't even asked for another date. But the way he had looked at her . . . He was interested. She had to try it. She hadn't only herself to offer Carlos in some faraway place. She had twenty-four thousand dollars. That was an inconsiderable price to pay for Carlos. For she knew that no other man would ever excite her and thrill her and drive her wild as Carlos did. . . .

At ten o'clock the next morning Bernice entered the Citizen's Bank. She went directly across the shining floor to Carlos Brandon's wicket. She shoved another hundred-dollar bill through to him.

He grinned at the money and met her eyes. Something happened to his handsome face. Bernice would have sworn he looked relieved. Absolutely pleased. She flushed. At least that look was not simulated. It was real. He had been looking for her!

It frightened her, making her want to run. Bernice had

spent twenty-four years running from attention. But it made her weak with pleasure, too.

He counted out the change, leaning close to the wicket.

"Look," he whispered. "I'm taking the rest of the day off, Bernice. Got a headache. Sure hate to be alone the way my head is splitting. It's too bad you got to work."

She flushed. "But I don't. That's why I came for change. I'm taking the day off, too. I was going shopping."

She'd known she shouldn't have come with another hundred-dollar bill. There was still a chance the serial numbers might be traced to some crooked business. But her need to see Carlos had won.

"I'll meet you at the café," he said. "As soon as I can get relieved here. O.K.?"

She smiled at him. "I'm on my way there now."

Bernice looked up when Carlos sat across the café booth from her.

"I'm sorry about your headache," she said.

"What headache?" Carlos said. "I just had a nice time with you last night, Bernice. Believe me, my life has been no bed of nosegays these last weeks. It was swell to be around someone like you. I thought it would be fun to spend the day with you."

It was a casual statement, and he said it casually. But Bernice felt the hot sting of pleasurable tears.

"Why do you like me?" she said.

"What do you mean?"

"Oh, I—I'm certainly not pretty." She tried to laugh. "Why, I'm not even as pretty as you are."

He was watching her. He wasn't smiling. "You look all right to me," he said. "You look swell."

She shook her head. "I know how I look."

"Gee. You shouldn't run yourself down like that. It makes me sound pretty bad. It makes it sound like I have no taste. You shouldn't ever tell a man who likes you that you aren't pretty, Bernice. That's like telling him he can't pick 'em."

She laughed. That was the nicest thing anyone had ever said to her.

He dropped four lumps of sugar into his coffee and drank

it down hurriedly. He looked up. "If you don't think you're pretty enough to suit yourself," he said, "why don't you take one of those hundred-dollar bills you're always haunting me with and go down to Gloria Soonin's?"

"On Fifth Avenue?"

"Well, I said you sure don't have to. You look swell to me. It's just that Gloria Soonin makes human beings look like movie stars and movie stars look human. I knew a woman once who went to Soonin's. Boy, they know everything there is to know about beauty there. But like I said, why waste the money? You look swell."

Bernice's heart was thudding. She pushed open the thick doors of Gloria Soonin's Fifth Avenue salon and stepped into its air-conditioned sumptuousness. She felt lost and out of place, standing plain and self-conscious in the deep-rugged elegance. Even when they welcomed her, Bernice went on feeling nervous. Even when they admitted her into Gloria Soonin's private office, she felt no better.

Gloria Soonin looked no more real than one of the wax figures that graced the windows of her mammoth beauty salon. Throughout the country, women used Gloria Soonin's lotions, creams, and powders in the hope that they would be as lovely as Gloria Soonin had been before she began using her own famous cosmetics.

Gloria's hair had once been radiantly blonde. It was now blondely radiant. Her flesh had the bloom of the rose, for that tired cliché is the only one with the solid truth in it. She regarded the girl across the desk.

"My dear Miss Harper," she said with her famous smile, "you've been neglecting yourself. Let's start with your eyes. Is it really necessary that your vision be corrected to a twenty-twenty rating?"

"I don't think so," Bernice said.

"A lot of women would rather not be able to see across the room than have to look through such plate glass as that," Gloria said. "Why don't you see a lens technician? If he thinks contact lenses wouldn't be adequate, try a light-weight pair of glasses with an upsweep that would accentuate the gaunt look of your face. We can't hide that, my dear, and since we can't, we might as well make the most of it."

Bernice nodded.

"And your hair," Gloria said. "Luckily for your gaunt face and split hair ends, style will permit us to give you a feather cut. You're going to find, Miss Harper, that your hair styling is going to do more for you than any other one thing."

Carlos was awaiting her when she came down the two steps into the café near the Citizen's Bank. He grinned and stared at her. Her heart beat faster. He's pleased, she thought. He likes the way I look. Even her dress had been chosen by the staff at Gloria Soonin's. It accentuated the slenderness of her hips. It straightened her shoulders, made them seem wider. It subtly suggested firm, high breasts. It was a youthful dress. It was so unquestionably right that just wearing it gave Bernice a new sense of self-confidence.

"Gee, you look swell," Carlos said. "I don't want you to think you didn't look fine before. But now you'll feel better, won't you?"

"Do you like me this way?"

"Sure."

"Then I feel wonderful."

"You look wonderful."

Bernice tried to keep her voice casual. "When we first met, Carlos, you said something I haven't been able to forget. About running away. Gee, I'd like to get out of this town."

"O.K.," Carlos said. "Let's take a bus ride somewhere. We can pretend we're running away."

She shook her head. "You're laughing. I didn't mean that. Something is wrong, Carlos, you won't ever talk about yourself. You don't tell me anything."

"What's there to tell, Bernice? A country boy. A job in the city. A pretty girl and broke. Why should I want to talk about that?"

"But that's not all. You never stay with me after seven o'clock."

"Is that terrible?"

"It is to me. Why must you run every day at seven? Why do you begin to get nervous and watch the clock?"

His face was set and angry. "Maybe I've something I have to do, Bernice."

"You act like you're in trouble. You won't tell me about it. You seem to like me. Looks like if you did, you'd tell me."

"There's nothing to tell. The best thing is to forget it."

"I can't."

His eyes were cold. "All right. What do you want me to do, stop seeing you altogether?"

Her mouth parted. "Oh, no. Please, Carlos. I didn't mean that. I won't argue again. I won't say anything. Not any more."

"Gosh, Bernice, I've skipped work four times to be with you, haven't I? What do I have to do?"

"I don't know. I'd just like to get away from here. Maybe across the Atlantic."

"Let's make it the Pacific," he said. "It's bigger."

They both laughed. Her hand was on the table. His fingers covered it. Bernice felt the tremors move up her arm and congeal in her throat, almost suffocating her. She turned her hand palm upward. She spread her fingers wide and taut, closing them over Carlos' like a vise. That was the way she wanted to hold him.

He looked at her. "Hey," he said. "Not here."

She was waiting for him the next morning outside the bank. He was taking the morning off again. He had called her and told her to meet him. She had run all the way.

She put out her hand and he took it. The need to touch him overwhelmed her now and they walked along the street with her clinging to his hand.

They were almost at the subway kiosk. Carlos stopped dead still in his tracks.

"Go on, Bernice." He spoke from the side of his mouth. His voice was frightened. "Go on, I tell you. Keep walking. Go home. I'll call you. I'll come to see you as soon as I can."

She stared at him. But he wasn't looking at her. His distended eyes were fixed on something across the wide walk. She followed the direction of his gaze.

A man was leaning against the fender of a highly glossed new Buick Riviera. He was tall, even taller than Carlos, but he was thin. Gaunt. His gaudy tie was knotted at the tight collar of a pearl-gray shirt. His gray suit had three-quarter-length coat and tight cuffed trousers. His fair-skinned face was pale; he looked as if he'd grown up in pool halls and never breathed anything but cue dust. He was manicuring his white nails with a penknife. He was staring at Carlos, face expressionless.

Bernice had no intention of leaving Carlos now unless she were bodily forced apart from him. She stood at his side. He seemed to have forgotten her.

"Hi, Mitch," Carlos said. His voice sounded hollow.

Mitch straightened up from the car. He came slowly across the walk. "Yesterday you was late," Mitch said.

"I told you. I—" Carlos began. But he seemed to know an alibi was useless. He gave it up with a slight shrug.

"Now today again you ain't workin' at all."

"All right! I'm not working."

"Why?"

"I've got a headache."

"Another one?" Mitch looked at Bernice. He motioned toward the car. "If you ain't doing anything, Carlos, why don't you come along with me? Sure like to talk to you."

Carlos opened his mouth to protest. His shoulders sagged. "All right," he said. He turned to Bernice. "It was swell. I—I'll see you again."

Mitch looked at Bernice again. He said, "Don't take no bets on it, baby."

Carlos tried to smile at her. But his face was pale and taut.

Bernice stood and watched him get in the glossy car and drive away with the man he had called Mitch. And what about the day they were going to spend together? Her heart sank. When will I see him again?

She walked through the busy streets to her apartment. In her room she kicked off her shoes. She raked the upsweep glasses from her eyes. She drew back her arm as though she were going to hurl them through the window.

She cast off the pretty new dress and wandered about the place in her slip. She ate a lunch of tomato soup and crackers. All the money she had spent to look lovely enough for Carlos—what good was it doing her? What was the matter? What was he afraid of? Where was he?

The telephone rang. She leaped up from the divan, praying it was Carlos.

It was her mother. Bernice half listened to her chatter. A million things, Bernice thought, that I'm not interested in at all. Her mother said, "The funniest thing, Bernice. A man was asking about you this morning. Early. Before seven o'clock this morning."

Fred Findlay. That was Bernice's first thought.

"Was it a detective?" she said.

"Oh, no," said her mother. "This was a young man. Real good-looking, Bernice. Blond. Tall. I've seen movie stars at the RKO that couldn't even touch him."

Bernice frowned. She felt empty in her stomach. Carlos. Before seven in the morning.

"What did he want, Ma?"

"I don't know. He just asked what you were doing, where you worked. Who you used to work for." Her mother's laugh was self-deprecating. "I hope you don't mind, Bernice. I talked my silly head off, he seemed so interested. And so good-looking."

Bernice replaced the telephone. She began to tremble. Maybe they'd been watching her since she cashed that first hundred-dollar bill. Good God, she had been about to tell Carlos all about the twenty-four thousand dollars!

Anger made her ill. Wouldn't that have been lovely! A trap baited with someone as terrific as Carlos Brandon!

What a fool you were! the voices screeched inside her. What a fool! Don't you know you can't trust anyone now? Now less than ever! You've got to stay alone now. That's part of the price you have to pay for getting what you wanted.

Bernice strode about the room. Getting what she wanted? What had she got that she wanted? She wanted only one thing. She wanted to be appreciated, admired, loved. Well, she was farther from it than ever.

She hated Carlos. She no longer even wanted to live, she hated him so terribly. She thought, I only want to see him one more time I only want to tell him what I think of him.

The doorbell rang. She wasn't even going to answer it. There was no one in the world she wanted to see. She even took a perverse pleasure in listening to its ringing. She sat on the side of her bed, her dry eyes wide, her hair rumpled, listening to it ring.

"Bernice!"

It was Carlos. All the hatred, all the despair washed out of her. She ran toward the door in her slip, her hair wild.

She flung open the door.

He smiled at her. There it was. That look of relief in his face again!

"Hello," he said.

She just stared at him. He stepped inside and let the door close behind him. He waited only until the lock clicked. He caught her to him, his arms lifting her into place against him.

She could feel the warmth of him and the strength of him and the excitement of him. She began to tremble in his arms. Her teeth were chattering when he kissed her. But his mouth closed over hers, and his tongue thrust deep in her mouth. She grabbed his head in her hands, dragging him closer, feeling his tongue thrusting deeper. . . .

"I've been so afraid for you all day."

"Don't be, Bernice. It was just a guy I owe some money to. I came as quick as I could, Bernice."

"I'm glad." She tilted her head and kissed him again, her parted mouth clinging. Her fingers dug into his back. She drew away, talking against his mouth. "Why'd you do it, Carlos? Why'd you go up there? Asking questions about me?"

She felt him go tense. A frown moved across his face. His eyes narrowed. "Why do you think I did?"

"I don't know."

He laughed. "I was up that way, Bernice. I had to be up early. I had an errand up there. I went around to where you grew up. I was thinking about you. And I happened to meet your mother. And there it is. I'm sorry. I didn't think you'd mind."

"Mind?" she said through her tears. "I don't mind, Carlos. Even if I did mind, I couldn't help it. I couldn't stay away from you."

He carried her across to the divan, held her in his arms. "It does happen that way, Bernice. Two people meet. They know. Right from the start."

64

"I couldn't believe it was like that with you."

"It was, though. I couldn't get you out of my mind."

"I threw myself at you. I wanted you so. That first day."

"You didn't! Sure you wanted me to love you. I wanted it, too. Only I want something better than that for us, Bernice."

She felt her heart slugging. This was a dream. It wasn't real. In a moment, the pool. The mushrooms.

He was holding an inexpensive necklace before her.

"On the way to work," he said, "I saw this in a jewelry store. It looked like you, Bernice. I wanted you to have it." He snapped it about her throat.

She couldn't speak. At last she whispered. "You shouldn't. You can't afford it."

"What the hell?" Carlos scoffed. "Who wants to eat?" She buried her face against his shoulder. When he spoke, his voice was grim. "You know what I wish, Bernice? I wish we could be married."

"Married?"

"Oh, I know it's crazy. But crazy or not, it's what I want."

"But you don't know anything about me."

"I know I love you. Do you know anything about me?"

She laughed. "No. But that's different. I don't care." Her fingers dug into him. "The only thing I hate," she said, "is that we'll have to wait two whole days for the license."

"You're supposed to laugh, Bernice. I don't make enough money to marry on."

"Maybe I make enough," she whispered.

His voice was sarcastic. "I don't want my wife to work. Any more than I want to live in this town with her. I'd like to clear out of here, just you and me. Now. Today."

She sat up, taking his beautiful face in her hands. "Don't get mad, now," she pleaded. "But I have some money, Carlos. And I've never loved anyone as I do you."

"Now you're kidding me. And I wasn't kidding, Bernice."

She caught her breath. "I'm not. I'm trying to tell you. I'll lend you the money. Tell me where we'd go. Tell me!"

"Florida?"

She sighed. "All right. We'll go. Next week."

"Next week? Why not next year? Why not never? You're not anxious—"

"Anxious?" She laughed. "I just didn't want to frighten you."

His voice was ironic. "I'll bet we could get reservations on a plane today. We'd be in Florida in four hours. No damned two-day wait down there. We could be married tomorrow."

She was clinging to his shoulders with white-knuckled hands. "I'll call," she whispered. "If we can get a reservation, we'll do it."

He sat there watching her.

Bernice was trembling as she picked up the telephone.

Chapter Eight

They were in Florida that night. They arrived at the Tampa International Airport at six o'clock.

Bernice was tense and sick with nervous anxiety. She had packed hurriedly, and it was on her mind all during the flight that she had no nightgown. She even managed to find time to plan the kind of nightgown she would buy. She hoped the stores wouldn't be closed when they arrived in Florida. All she knew about Florida was that it was the city of Miami surrounded by swamps, alligators, and cotton-haired old Negro men singing in the cotton fields. She even doubted they had stores where they sold lace nightgowns. And that added to her nervous tension.

She had given Carlos three hundred dollars before they left her small apartment. The tickets cost just over a hundred. He had said nothing about returning any of the remaining money. But she had Carlos. She didn't care about money.

When they came off the plane, Bernice said, "Let's get a cab, Carlos. I want to get into town before all the stores close."

"Why?"

"I want to buy something."

"Look, Bernice. You're all right. Just the way you are, you're all right. We don't want to stay here. This town is too big. We're going to get a bus out of here right away."

"Please, Carlos. It won't take five minutes."

His jaw tightened. But he managed to keep his voice light. "Look, honey. You're marrying me. I'm going to be boss in this family. O.K.?"

"Yes, but—"

"All right. We're moving on. Listen, baby, there are hotels on the beaches. And the beaches are really white. You can look for miles and see white sand. Not the yellow, oily stuff you saw at Coney. Real white sand. That's where we're going. Some nice quiet beach hotel. O.K. with you?"

"Gee. It sounds wonderful, Carlos."

"Then stop arguing about a store."

They hurried toward the taxi stands. Carlos was carrying both their small bags. He leaned in the front window of a cab. "How much to the bus station, fella?"

"Be three bucks, mister. You and the lady and the bags."

Bernice saw Carlos wince. She smiled lovingly. He hated to spend her money foolishly.

"All right," he decided. "If that's the way it is."

There wasn't a bus out of town for an hour and a half. They ate supper at a small table in the bus-station restaurant. Carlos ordered for them. When the meal was brought, he began to eat ravenously. He didn't even look up from his plate.

Bernice smiled. He was hungry. The excitement had affected them differently. Bernice could only pick at her food. Carlos pushed his empty plate back and sat watching her.

"What's the matter?" he said. "Not hungry?"

"Not very, I guess." She smiled wanly at him. "Too excited."

"You mean you're not going to eat your dinner?"

Bernice looked at the steaming plate. She might have taken a few more bites. Maybe if they sat there long enough, she might eat it all.

"If you don't want it," he said, "give it here. There's no use wasting it, is there?"

He reached over and took away her plate. She pulled her coffee before her and began to sip it. She lifted her eyes from her cup. Carlos was already finishing off her meal.

The waitress was standing beside him. "I'll take apple

pie," he told her. "You want any dessert, Bernice?"

"It comes with the meal," the waitress said.

"Well, sure, bring it, then," Carlos said. "No use wasting it."

Carlos finished both slices of pie. He picked up the check and went over it carefully. He looked up.

"You have two cups of coffee?"

Bernice nodded.

"Oh," he said. "Well, you have to be careful in these places. They'll take you. Know you'll never be back."

He stood up. He took change from his pocket. Bernice saw him touch a quarter, then obviously change his mind. He reluctantly pushed a dime under the corner of his plate. Bernice thought he was sweet, trying to save her money like that.

It was almost nine o'clock when they arrived in Clearwater. They walked five blocks before Carlos found a hotel with rates to suit him. When they had their room, he got a telephone book. He found the county clerk's office. By much telephoning, he was able to get in touch with Carrie Newson, a clerk in the license bureau. Finally he hung up and smiled at Bernice. "O.K.," he said. "Let's go get married."

For Bernice there hadn't been any moment before this one. She was floating on clouds of velvety bubbles. She moved beside Carlos without knowing where they went or whom they saw. She knew the clerk was a stout woman who thought Carlos beautiful and so droll. There were baby diapers spread over everything in the front room of the clerk's house. She called in a couple of neighbors for witnesses. Everybody took it calmly except Bernice. The civil ceremony was quick, cheap, and shoddy. Bernice had dreamed of a church and an organ's muted music, a minister's hushed voice. But she wouldn't have changed anything. She heard Carlos say, "I will." She heard her own voice from some distant place saying, "I will, I will." And they were laughing at her. And it was over. They were back in their hotel room. And Bernice wished for a lace nightgown.

Carlos undressed casually before her distended eyes. She knew with a twinge of jealousy that Carlos was accustomed to undressing before girls. He had done it so often that they were all one and all the same, and it was so casual that it never occurred to him that she was any different than all the others.

She sat in the uncomfortable hotel chair. Her lips were parted. Her feather-cut hair was damp across her forehead. She couldn't take her eyes from him as he undressed. The strength went out of her, and she sat limply staring at him. She saw the muscles bulge across his wide shoulders. His tanned chest was lightly dusted with short dark hairs. His belly was corded with muscles and was naturally sucked in over his slender waist. He dropped his trousers and kicked them to a chair. His underpants were green and orange.

He turned and looked over his shoulder at her. "Hey. You gonna sit there all night?"

"Carlos—" her voice was a whisper. She was staring at him. "Carlos—"

He frowned. "What's the matter with you?"

"Carlos—" She lifted her hand toward him, but it was trembling so badly that she dropped it again. "Carlos—"

She managed to push herself up from the chair. She put out her arms. He took a step toward her, still watching her oddly. When her icy hands touched the warmth of his solid, muscular arms, she wilted against him.

"For God's sake, Bernice!"

She was dead weight. With his hands on her back, he tried to support her. But she slid down, her lips raking his body as she crumpled. She caught her arms about his legs and buried her fevered face against him. "I love you," she whispered. "I love you. I love you."

"Then get up. Get undressed, honey."

"I can't, Carlos. I can't get up."

"What are you saying? What's the matter with you?"

She brushed away her glasses, the glamour glasses suggested by Gloria Soonin, and looked up at him beseechingly. "I can't get up. Laugh at me. Anything. Only I can't get up. You'll have to help me."

His face twisted into an angry snarl. "What is this? What kind of dodge is this?"

"Be patient, Carlos!" she pleaded. "Be patient. Help me up. Help me up, darling. Pick me up."

He bent over and picked her up easily in his arms. She laughed a little and clung to him. "Take me to bed," she said.

He carried her to the bed. "Now. Tell me," he said. "What's the matter?"

She stared up at him and began to cry. "Don't you know what's the matter? I can't move. I love you. I can't move. You must help me, Carlos."

He clutched up the front of her dress to lift her. Her shoulders came upward a half foot or so, and her head flopped back. "Damn it!" he growled. "Damn you!"

Her dress tore in his fist. Angered, he ripped it away.

"Yes!" she whispered. "Yes. Yes. Yes."

He tore off her bra and her panties. She reached up for him and pulled him down upon her. He fought to get free, but her arms were like steel wires. Some of the terrible desire in her communicated itself to him. With passion that was more like anger than love, he thrust her back on the bed. But his passion was no match for hers. The violence in his green eyes only stirred her more. When he tried to fall away from her, she moaned at him. "No, Carlos, no. Don't stop, Carlos! Please!"

"My God, I've got to!" he gasped. "Don't you know anything?"

"I can't help it!" she wailed. "I can't help it, Carlos. You must! Please, Carlos. Please!"

"Let go, Bernice," he said. His voice was sharp. "Let me go. I'll hit you. So help me God, I'll hit you."

For a moment, her breath rasping across her taut lips, she clung to him, her face twisted with hatred. Abruptly she released him and fell back against the pillow.

He lay above her and looked at her. Her breasts heaved as she breathed heavily. Her nipples were tense, pointing. She had turned her face away and buried it in the bed covers. He could hear her muffled sobbing. He touched her shoulders, but she shook his hand away.

He sat on the edge of the bed, naked, and lighted a cigarette. He tried to be a man of the world about it.

"My God, Bernice," he said, making it all a joke. "You'd kill me if I let you."

She didn't answer. Finally he snuffed out the cigarette.

70

He glanced impatiently over his shoulder. She was still stretched tense and white beside him on the bed. For a long time he wouldn't hear her breathing, and then he would hear a short, indrawn sob.

His eyes bitter, he snapped off the light and lay down in the darkness beside her. There were few sounds in the small-town night. The silence itself was immense and hurting against his eardrums. He reached out, got his trousers from the chair, and touched the fold of bills in his pocket. He grinned contentedly, tossed the trousers back to the chair. In ten minutes he was snoring.

Bernice listened to his snores for what seemed hours. Finally, she too slept. And for the first time since Lloyd's death, she was able to sleep dreamlessly.

When she woke up, it was just daylight. She turned over in bed and looked at Carlos, the muscular, perfect body sprawled out on the bed, the tousled curly head on the pillow.

Maybe it'll be better, she told herself miserably. Maybe next time I won't be so crazy. But she knew better. The sight of his body, the touch of his hand would always excite her in a terrible, wonderful way that wasn't ever going to be quickly sated.

She shivered.

He was always going to drive her crazy with desire. And he was never going to be able to satisfy her.

Oh, God, she thought. Oh, God!

Chapter Nine

She stood it as long as she could. Her breathing was quick and short, and seemed to blast across her parted lips. She felt that she couldn't stand it, lying there looking at Carlos' bare body on the bed beside her.

Carlos continued to snore. She lay beside him, looking at the way the sparse hairs grew across his muscled chest.

She wanted to touch him, feel him. But she was afraid of what he might think if she woke him up and he found her almost sick at her stomach with wanting him.

71

She wriggled on the bed, needing to press herself against him. She had to hold her arms rigid at her sides to keep from putting her hands on him.

She watched him wake up. He rolled over, flopped on his back. He stretched his arms, yawning. Bernice's mouth was cottony. She stared.

He looked at her. "What time is it?" he said.

"I don't know," she said. "It's early. Real early."

"You hungry?"

"No, Carlos. No. Are you?"

"God, yes. This gulf air makes you hungry first thing in the morning. Usually I can't eat a thing right when I wake up. But I'm hungry now."

"Let's not eat yet," she said. "Please, let's not eat yet."

Frowning, he rolled over and looked at her. Their eyes met. She watched it happen. She saw him begin to want her, responding to the heat in her, the need for him, the desire that made her breathless and pale.

He grinned at her. "Hey," he said. His voice was low. "Hey."

He reached out, digging his hands into her hair, pulling her down.

That was all Bernice wanted. That was all she'd been waiting for. She drove herself in upon him. Her hands dug into him, her fingernails raked him, her teeth sank into him. He cursed her. But the curses were like tender caresses. He tried to thrust her away and then he was dragging her in closer, holding her tighter, cutting off her breath, strangling her, and she didn't give a damn.

That day they left Clearwater and took a cottage on the gleaming beach south of Indian Rocks. Carlos seemed to be searching for a particular kind of place. They kept moving until he found it. The Rockledge Motel pleased him, and that puzzled Bernice, because the rental was ninety dollars a week. She knew already that Carlos didn't like to spend money that well. But there was something about the rate, the cottages, the surroundings that was just what he was seeking. She had never seen him so pleased with himself.

She wanted to ask him what was the matter, what hounded him, what was he running from? But that other thing, the fact that Carlos couldn't satisfy her, was already an unspeakable matter between them. She didn't want any more trouble. She was sure things were going to be all right once they settled down, once they got acquainted.

Besides, the island pleased and excited Bernice, the brightly colored cottages that laced the narrow fingers of land. There were many islands, locked together by hump-backed bridges on which sun-baked fishermen crawled like ants. A narrow black highway wound from the top island to the tip of the last one. All day long it was crowded and loud with cars. On the bay side fishermen dozed in row-boats, and in the gulf sleek women sunbathed on the decks of yawls and sloops and yachts. Children hunted snails or screamed in the shallows along the endless stretches of white sand and green water and dazzling sun.

It was all a million miles from the dingy house where Lloyd Deerman had died. It was a place of brilliance and light and warmth. It was going to be heaven for her and Carlos. They didn't have to run any more. This was far enough. All they had to do was settle the trouble between them, and everything was going to be swell.

The first night they went swimming. It was after eleven o'clock, and the beach was silent except for the rumbling of the waves. Lights winked along the horizon and cars zipped past on the highway. They swam out past the sand bar into the darkness. Bernice caught her breath. When she lifted her arms out of the water, light poured off of them.

"Phosphorus," Carlos told her. She watched him swing his arms in wide bright circles under the water. "Swim around, you'll glow."

They slid out of their bathing suits and swam together, like yellow flames under the water. They were like kids and Bernice knew they were going to be happy now. God, how could people help being happy in a place like this?

But that night Carlos was sleepy when he staggered into the cottage. He fell across the bed and was asleep before she had creamed her face. That night Bernice had a dream. And it was hellish, because Lloyd Deerman was drowning, falling and rolling and twisting in water bright with phos-phorus. And the hell of it was that even though he was fall-ing in the water, Bernice could hear the splintering crack of the stair railings and nothing could save her from that sound.

Near their cottage was an odd-shaped green building that was the community shopping center. Before it curved a wide green sidewalk shaded by palms and bordered by crotons and cacti and running lantana. In the modernistic stores was sold every kind of merchandise. There was even a movie theatre and a small exclusive bar.

And there was a dress shop. It was run by a swish named Elhanner. There was one thing that Elhanner understood. He knew all there was to know about what clothes a woman of any shape or size should wear.

Bernice walked in, and, hypnotized by the beautiful clothes, she spent almost five hundred dollars before Carlos could drag her out of there.

Her eyes gleamed at the styles Elhanner brought out for her to see. She didn't notice how silent Carlos became as she began to spend money. He sat and watched her. She thought about the grim look in his beautiful face only in passing.

Elhanner was making a play for Carlos' attentions. She shuddered. Carlos was angry because the fairy was preening before him.

Carlos said nothing until they were outside the shop. They were walking along the palm-fringed green sidewalk. She heard his breath exhale.

"My God, Bernice," Carlos said. "What are you trying to do, buy everything in that goddamned Good Fairy's shop?"

"They're so beautiful," Bernice said. "And he's so right about everything I should wear." She didn't tell Carlos that Soonin's had given her a short, compact course in selecting clothes. "Elhanner knows more about clothes than I ever will."

"You've got more stuff than you can ever wear," Carlos said. "Now let's stop going in there!"

She smiled. "You don't have to go any more unless you want to, Carlos. I know he makes you uncomfortable."

He looked at her, his mouth twisting. "Elhanner doesn't make me uncomfortable. If he goes crazy enough about me, I ought to be worth plenty to him."

"Carlos!"

"All right. You asked me. I'm telling you. A queer going nuts over me is no worse than some dames I've had to put up with."

"Carlos. Stop talking like that. It's indecent. It makes me sick."

"Maybe you think it didn't make me sick, seeing you spend money like that!" he snarled.

She sighed. "It's my money, Carlos."

"O.K.! It's your money. You don't have to rub that in. So now I'm not even supposed to say anything about the way you throw it away, O.K., spend it any way you want to!"

"Carlos, I'm sorry. I won't buy any more clothes. There were a couple of things I wanted. But I won't get them."

"Sure. Get 'em. It's your money. You've told me so. Sure, I'm not working."

"I don't want you to work."

"Sure, I came down here on your money! It's your money that I eat on, that I sleep on. Sure. Spend it any way you want to."

She caught his arm. "Carlos. Please don't be angry. It's just that there were so many things I wanted. Believe it or not, I've never had the things I wanted. Just like you're the first person I ever loved, this is the first time I've ever been in a place like this. It's like a dream. This is the first time I've ever seen so many lovely things. I know you're just trying to take care of me, and just trying to take care of my money. I'm glad, darling. I'll let you. It makes me feel good to know you're taking care of me."

"If I'm going to take care of you, let me. Stay out of that fairy's store."

"I only want to look nice so you'll love me!"

He threw open the cottage door and strode in. "Spending money like that is no way to make me love you."

"Why are you so mad because I spent a little money?"

"A little money! Five hundred dollars! Just don't expect me to like it."

"You don't want me to have *anything!*"

She spat that word at him. They knew she didn't mean clothes. They stared at each other. This was as near as Bernice had come to telling Carlos that he couldn't satisfy her.

75

They had known it, but as long as they didn't talk about it, they could pretend.

He was pale. "All right. Leave me, then."

Leave him? She shook her head slowly. She hadn't meant that. God knew she'd only been trying to strike back at him.

She ran to him. She slid to her knees, pressing her face against him. "I don't want to leave you. I don't know why I said that. I just don't want you mad with me. I couldn't stand it away from you. All I want is for you to love me. Love me. Hold me, Carlos, love me."

"No," he said. "I won't let you talk to me like that."

She buried her face against him. Her heart was pumping twice as fast as it should. She was wild for him. Even his anger excited her.

He pushed her away. "Let me alone," he said. "You think all you got to do is throw it at me and everything is O.K. You think just because it makes me hot to see you get so wild for it, all you got to do is go crazy."

"I don't go crazy," she said, shaking her head. "I don't, Carlos. You drive me crazy."

He stalked toward the bedroom. "I wouldn't let anybody get me down like that."

"Nobody gets me down. You get me down." She ran after him.

She pressed herself against him, feeling nothing but the excitement inside her, not even knowing how she was working her body against his.

He began to laugh and tried to push her away again. But Bernice knew. He had begun to respond. It didn't make any difference that it was nothing but the hell in her that got him.

She wanted to yell with laughter. She knew now. She could get him. She could always get him. She was the great-grandmother of every whore who ever lived. She knew all the lures. They were born in her. Better than anything else she knew the pull of raw hot passion for Carlos.

Her hands like talons, she grabbed the back of his head and jerked his mouth down against hers. His teeth cut her lips, thudded against her teeth.

"Damn you!" he snarled. "You damned little slut. Let me alone."

He pulled away from her. His swinging arm drove everything off the dresser. She didn't even hear the noise, the bottles and the combs and the jars clattering on the floor and rolling under the bed.

They fell against the dresser, pushing it away from the wall. They slid past it with Bernice dragging at him and pulling him down with her.

He wasn't fighting her now. He was fighting her clothes. He was pulling them off. She listened to them rip. Elhanner's expensive dress made a lovely expensive sound in Carlos' fists.

She could feel his fingers digging into her hair. She could feel his body growing hot, responding to her own abandoned hotness. She flung off her glasses as he pushed her back on the floor. She clawed her fingernails into his shoulders, sank her teeth into his throat, feeling the laughter mixing with the passion. She was going to have him. Now on the floor, like this. Even if it left her tormented, raving. Even if it drove her crazy. She had to have him.

She opened her eyes, staring across Carlos' shoulder. There they were, reflected in the tilted dresser mirror, like a fantastic painting of two abandoned beings lost in a passion that had nothing to do with love and was made of hatred.

Carlos. The hungry, driving anger of him, clutching at her throat and at her bare shoulders, hating her, looking as if he wanted to kill her.

And for the first time she saw her own face in the fire of wanting. Her sweated hair was pushed back from her face, her cheeks were drained of color, and her eyes were tortured with a torment that was sweet and unbearable at the same terrible moment.

She stared at this motion picture of herself, her hands raking at his shoulders, her mouth taut and red across her teeth.

She watched, fascinated. Carlos' frantic hands closed on her thighs, dragging her closer. The floor rattled, the mirror quavered, wavering like ripples on a pond. And when it was quiet, she was still staring at it, but it wasn't the same any more.

Carlos had fallen away from her. Her gaze lifted to her own eyes and she saw what she looked like when he left her crazy, writhing in her need for him, wanting him so badly her face was twisted and creased, ugly with wanting him.

The mounds of her breasts heaved, her hips still moved, her head rolled on the pillow of her black hair. He was spent. There was nothing he could do for her. Nothing he could do but hate her because she showed him how ineffectual he was.

What a hellish thing, she thought, staring at the girl in that mirror. The passion in her was always going to rouse Carlos, but all he was ever going to be able to do was carry her to hell and leave her there. And every time it was going to be worse. Every time he'd hate her a little more for what she was doing to his pride. And he'd go on hating her until his hatred was as hideous as her insatiable need for him.

"Try," she pleaded. "Try, Carlos!"

"My God, Bernice. I can't. Maybe later. Maybe I can later."

Her head stopped rolling. Her breath subsided. "All right," she said. But she said it without hope.

Chapter Ten

Forty minutes later, Carlos came out of the bathroom. Bernice was lying on the bed, staring at the ceiling.

He was showered, immaculate in sport shirt, white trousers, and strap sandals. "Let's go to lunch," he said. "Do you want to go eat, Bernice?"

She turned her head and looked at him. The thought of food sickened her. But there was no choice, really. She had to go with Carlos or be left alone in this cottage. She couldn't stand the thought of being alone.

He flopped on the divan in the front room and waited until she was dressed. They walked across the highway to the restaurant.

He held his head up and swaggered a little as he walked. But he said nothing to Bernice. She held his arm as they crossed the air-conditioned room toward a booth. She wanted to tell him that it was her fault, that she didn't care if he satisfied her or not. But she knew better than that. She couldn't even mention it. She had to find something to talk about that was safe, yet something that would let him know that she loved him, she forgave him, she wanted him.

"Do you like the green color of these walls?" she said.

"Yeah, Yeah. Swell." He shook free of her hand.

She sat across the table from him. She whispered, "I'm sorry, Carlos. I've said I'm sorry. Please stop acting this way."

She put her hand on the table, waited until he covered it. She pressed a hundred-dollar bill into his palm.

He drew his hand away, shoved it into his trousers pocket. He grinned at her. "O.K., Bernice. Don't you worry. It's going to be better for us."

She laughed. "I don't care. I love you."

He nodded. "Sure you do. What red-blooded American girl could resist me?"

"Never mind the red-blooded girls," she said. "You've got to be content with me."

She reached across the table and straightened his tie. She just couldn't keep her hands off him.

The blonde waitress was standing by the table. Her smile was disdainful. Carlos jerked his head back, moving away from Bernice. He ordered for them, and when the waitress was gone he leaned across the table toward Bernice.

"For God's sake, Bernice. Can't you keep your hands off me in public?"

She stared at him. "What do you care what a waitress thinks?"

"I don't care," he replied. "I don't care about her at all. It's you, Bernice. Why do you think she was smiling like that?"

"I don't even care why."

"Well, it just so happens that I do care."

"Why don't you apologize to her when she brings your steak?"

"I told you. It's not her I care about. It's what she was thinking. What people think about you. Not just her—

everybody who sees you acting the way you do!"

"How am I acting? Like I'm in love? Shouldn't I act that way? I am in love, you know. With you. I don't care who knows."

"You don't act like you're in love," he answered. "You act starved. Plain starved, Bernice."

Her carefully drawn red mouth went lax. Starved? Of course she was. Months and years—a lifetime of starvation, of wanting to be loved, of wanting a man like Carlos. And then to have him. To find he resented the money she spent on herself, to find that he was ashamed of the fact that she loved him so terribly. To know that he was never going to be able to satisfy her desire for him. A desire that left her weak when he touched her hand. A desire that no other man could arouse so terribly. A desire that was always going begging, starving. . . .

After breakfast the next day they went out to lie on the beach.

Carlos slept under a green-striped umbrella and Bernice rolled like mutton on a spit, browning evenly under the sun. She tried to talk with Carlos, but he wouldn't answer her. She lay with her head on her arms, feeling the sun cooking the drops of sweat into her body. She knew she was frying, she was hot enough to sizzle, and yet she was cold.

She fell asleep. She awakened suddenly and sat up on her blanket. The sun was halfway down the sky. And Carlos was gone.

She looked about, searching the beach and the water.

He was nowhere in sight. Maybe he'd gone to the cottage. But she couldn't escape the fact that it had been morning when they came out on the beach. It was now late afternoon.

Feeling dizzy and sick at her stomach, she got up and dragged the sandy blanket after her across the beach. She tried to walk slowly, but she wanted to run.

She dropped the blanket at the front door of her bright little cottage. The door was closed. The key was in the receptacle beside it. She called, "Carlos."

Her fingers trembled as she forced the key into the lock. She flung open the door and went in the living room. There was a trail of sand across the rug. Carlos had been here.

She padded into the bedroom. She found his bathing trunks wadded on the floor of the shower. She stepped into the shower, pulled the curtain, and turned on the water. The spray struck her like needles. She knew she was burned crisp. The cold water made her so ill she was nauseated.

She staggered out of the shower. Her fiery skin felt icy under her fingers. She tried to put on a slip and bra, but she couldn't stand the touch of them against her flesh.

She stared at herself in the mirror. She was burned a fiery red brown across her shoulders and legs. Her face was deeply burned except where her sunglasses had covered her eyes.

She bit back a scream.

For one terrible moment, she thought she was going to faint.

Those were Lloyd's white, sightless eyes staring out of that dark-burned face!

"Carlos!"

She clenched her fists at her sides and ran away from the mirror. She managed to wriggle into her pants and she found a strapless dress. She slipped her seared feet into a pair of slippers. Why had Carlos left her to burn in the sun like this?

She went out of the cottage, leaving the front door standing open. The sun was painful on her blistered shoulders. But she knew she couldn't stand it another minute away from Carlos. She had to find him.

The manager of the motel was watering flowers at the entrance. He was a stout, gray-haired man who had retired from business in Iowa and got rich in Florida renting his beach cottages.

"Have you seen my husband?" Bernice said.

He looked at her. "You better see a doctor, Mrs. Brandon. You got a bad case of sunburn."

"Yes," she said. "Yes. Have you seen Carlos?"

He shook his head, frowning at the anxiety in her voice. "No, I haven't," he said.

Bernice was sure he was lying. She tried not to care that he lied, tried to keep her voice light. "Oh, well, he probably went to dinner without me."

"Yes, ma'am," the court owner said. "If you'll tell me what time you'll be back in your cottage, Mrs. Brandon, I'll call the doctor and have him drop in."

Bernice shook her head. "I don't know."

She hurried away. She went across the blistered highway, feeling the sun on her shoulders like the blast from a furnace. She stopped at the door of the restaurant and looked in.

Her eyes met those of the blonde waitress. Bernice hated her. The girl seemed to know that Bernice was frightened, that Carlos was gone, and that Bernice was running around looking for him. Her smile was superior. Bernice moved on.

She saw him sitting in the cool bar. He looked up and saw her coming through the door. There was no pleasure in his face. She saw that he'd been drinking for a long time. There were fifteen or twenty squares of paper on the bar before him. Each one had a single number scrawled on it.

"Hi," he said. "I'm glad you came." His voice was slurred. "You'll have to pay for my last drink. I'm broke."

She stared at him, opened her mouth to speak. She'd given him a hundred-dollar bill only yesterday. Something in his eyes warned her not to mention that. She closed her lips and nodded.

Carlos smiled. Triumph made his face smug. She laid a twenty-dollar bill on the bar.

"Fix me another one," Carlos said. Bernice sat on the stool beside him. "Dugan, I want you to meet my wife. This is Dugan, Bernice. He knows what I want. He can fix it for me."

Bernice glanced at the bartender. He snapped off the radio on the shelf behind the bar. He was a short, squash-faced man with dark curly hair. He grinned at her.

"You got a lovely husband, Mrs. Brandon," he said. "He didn't hit one all afternoon. Right now he's a little high and a little mad about it."

"Don't apologize for me," Carlos said. His voice was loud. "So I had a bad streak. I'll make it up." He sat up straight and looked at Bernice. "My God," he said. "What's happened to you?"

Bernice was feeling cold prickles through the crisp burn of her skin. She began to be cold all over. Her teeth chattered and her body began to shake.

"She's got a lulu of a sunstroke, mister!" Dugan said.

He fixed something green in a small glass and came around the bar. "Here, drink this," he said to Bernice. He looked at Carlos as Bernice drank. "You know how to dial a telephone, sonny?"

"Just because you got all my money, quit being so sweet to me," Carlos told him. "What's a doctor's number?"

"It's written in pencil right over the phone," Dugan said.

Dugan helped Bernice to a booth. "Don't lean back," he warned. "That leather'll feel cool, but when you try to get up, you'll think it's peeling your skin off. Soon as Personality over there gets the doctor, he can take you home."

Bernice's teeth were still chattering. She looked at the bartender, frowning. "Why do you talk about Carlos like that?" she whispered.

He smiled at her. "How long have you been married to him, honey?"

"Four days," she chattered.

"Four days," he repeated. "Imagine that. Four long unhappy days. You poor thing. You poor sunburned little thing."

Carlos half carried Bernice to the cottage. As they went in the front door, the doctor arrived in a yellow Cadillac convertible. Carlos went out to meet him.

Bernice sat on the edge of a chair. Her teeth were not chattering any more, but she was having a chill under the outer layer of her fried flesh. Her head ached and spun so she was giddy.

Sitting there, she could see the way Carlos looked at that convertible. His eyes had a hungry look, like a little boy yearning after a bicycle in a shop window. The kind of hunger she'd always had, only for something different.

The doctor came in, and after a moment Carlos followed.

The doctor was young, slightly older than Carlos. No one would ever call him handsome. He looked at Bernice, led her into the bedroom.

He prescribed for Bernice, put her in a soda bath, and when she was naked on her bed he spread a film of ointment over her burned flesh. Bernice sighed. The fire seemed to die out almost at once, leaving her weak and sleepy.

She heard the doctor talking to Carlos. "You'll get that prescription filled. I want you to put this ointment on her as I did, as she needs it and in the morning. Just don't try to get too near her or touch her and she'll be all right. The ointment will take the fire out, and she should be able to sleep."

Bernice went to sleep. When she woke up, it was dusk.

"Carlos?"

The cottage was silent.

She lay miserable on the bed. She couldn't go out looking for him now. Some of the ointment had rubbed off on the sheets and the exposed places burned. She hoped he would hurry and rub the ointment on her burns. She got the jar and tried to reach the sorest places herself. She put the jar under her pillow, feeling better just because the soothing cream was so near.

She lay there and told herself Carlos was at supper. He would bring her a sandwich or something when he returned.

The hours dragged. The motel court grew loud as people gathered outside on the shuffleboard courts and around the card tables. The sounds roared in from the busy highway. Radios blared in the other cottages. The gulf boomed up on the white sands and rolled hissing out again. The radios were cut off one by one until there was only haunting music she could barely hear. The shuffleboard courts went dark. The muted talk continued at the card tables. There were only a few cars on the highway, and even the waves seemed quieter on the beach. Bernice thought, I can't stand it alone. I'm afraid. When I'm alone, I'm afraid.

She heard the front door open and then bang shut. She heard Carlos stagger against a chair and knock it over. She heard him curse. "Damn lights!" he muttered. "Where lights?"

The lights flared on in the front room. A yellow oblong of it fell across Bernice. She wanted to laugh with the relief she felt. Carlos was home.

He stood in the door. "I lost some money," he said. "To Dugan. I told him you'd pay him in the morning. He said O.K. O.K.?" His tie was awry. His hair was mussed over his forehead. He stared at her. "Where I sleep?" he said.

She looked at him. She wanted him to sleep with her. The fever in her body made her need him worse than ever. She couldn't bear the rest of the night without him.

"I'll sleep in the front room," he mumbled. He turned around, knocking over an end table. She heard it clatter to the floor. The front-room light was snapped out. She heard the springs of the divan sag as he flopped upon it. In less than three minutes, she could hear his even snores.

She lay hot and miserable on the damp bed. How was she going to sleep alone and needing him? But the sound of his snoring was comforting. At least he was home. At least he was near. Her eyes grew heavy. Her last thought was that she was feverish. She fell asleep.

It began at once, the loud splintering sound as Lloyd's body struck the stair railing. He went spinning down the steps. Fred Findlay was standing there to comfort him as he landed. Bernice stood at the head of the stairs, staring down at them. Finally Findlay lifted his head and met her gaze. Only his eyes were white. Slug-white, sightless. They bored into her. Lloyd's eyes. She wasn't ever going to be able to escape now because Fred Findlay had Lloyd's eyes!

She woke up screaming.

This time she knew she really screamed. The sound of it was echoing in her ears as she sat up on the bed. She saw lights come on in windows along the court.

Carlos stumbled into the bedroom and snapped on the light. He sank to the edge of the bed. "All right," he said. "What is it? What's the matter, Bernice?"

She drew away from him. His voice was sour and his breath was foul. She stared round-eyed at him, thankful for the light, thankful he was there. Her heart was still slugging against her ribs.

"A dream," she whispered. "It was awful. I was so frightened."

Carlos stared at her a moment. He shrugged, got a package of cigarettes from the table beside the bed, lighted one.

He stood up, exhaling a long puff of smoke. "Forget it," he advised. "Try to go back to sleep."

"Come to bed with me. Hold me."

"You know I can't. You're sunburned."

"I don't care!"

85

He started from the room.

"Where are you going?" she cried.

"Back to my wonderful bed, my bride," he said. "I know you got something on your mind, Bernice. Don't try to keep me up all night with it."

Her lips parted, she stared at him.

Something on her mind? How would Carlos know? How could he have found out? Her frightened eyes searched his face. She sank back against her pillow. Carlos didn't know. Carlos didn't care. He was just telling her he didn't give a damn about her woes, whatever they were.

"Please come back!" she pleaded.

"I told you. I'm going to bed."

"Come here, Carlos."

"I'm going to bed."

"Sleep with me. Hold me."

"You couldn't stand it." He stared at her seared body, the ointment glinting in the light, the outline where her bathing suit had been looking Easter-lily white against the fiery red of her legs and shoulders.

"I could stand it." Her febrile eyes clashed against his. "I can't stand it not having you."

She twisted on the bed and he watched her. Something happened to his face. She saw his eyes narrow, his mouth pull into a hard line. He started toward her on the bed. She knew he wanted to hurt her. Wanting to hurt her made him more passionate than he'd ever been, made his eyes as feverish as hers.

"It's going to hurt you," he told her. "It's going to hurt you." Only his voice didn't care. It rasped across his lips. He wanted to hurt her.

He fell against her. His arms went under her shoulders and she screamed with agony. It didn't stop him. The sound of her screaming drove him wilder. She felt as if the flesh were being raked from her back on the ridges of the rumpled sheets.

She heard something crash from the side of the bed. She was sobbing in pain and agony and delirium. And then she didn't care any more and he wasn't hurting her. He wasn't hurting her enough and the frantic chains of her arms tried to shackle him to her. But she wasn't strong enough, even in her fever and her need. He fought himself free.

She watched him stagger up to his feet and stand staring down at her, his eyes hating her.

"Carlos!" she cried. "My back, my shoulders! They're killing me. The ointment. Please. Rub it on me! It's here. I had it on the bed."

He looked down at the floor. "It's broke," he said. "It fell off the bed and broke."

"Use it anyway!"

"You can't. It's just a mess of salve and glass."

"I can't stand it. I'm burning up. It's killing me. I can't stand it."

She was on fire. It had never been so painful before. She couldn't even bear to lie on the rumpled sheet, and knowing there was no ointment made it worse.

"Looks like you'll have to stand it," Carlos said.

He snapped off the light as he stumbled back into the front room and left her moaning in the darkness, praying for morning.

Chapter Eleven

Her body was still afire at daylight and she hadn't slept. She lay on her stomach, praying Carlos would come in and smooth some of the lotion on her. Glass particles, anything, she didn't care any more. She wriggled to the edge of the bed and peered over the side. The lotion jar was smashed. It was a mess of glass and cream on the floor. She stretched out her fingers, hoping to get just a smear of it. She wanted just enough of it to cover the back of her neck where it felt as if somebody were pressing a smoldering coal against her bare skin. Her fingers trembled as she raked them across the top of the cream. She felt the sharp jab of a glass sliver and blood started to spread over the top of the white cream. She drew her hand away and sank back on the bed.

The doctor. Why in hell didn't Carlos get the doctor? How long did he think she could stand this?

She pushed up on her elbows and started to call him. She

heard him moving around in the bathroom, and, puzzled, she lay there with her mouth agape, listening. She sank back to the sheet. Carlos had been high last night. It wasn't like him to be up at this hour, even when he wasn't hung over.

Carlos came out of the bathroom. Bernice watched him from beneath lowered lids. Why was he up so early? He was shaved and dressed except for his shirt. He took one from the dresser drawer and slid his arms into it. He turned and looked at her. She let her lids close, feigning sleep.

He stuffed his shirt into his trousers. Her purse was on top of the dresser. She saw him glance at it. He selected a tie and knotted it about his throat and got a clean handkerchief. Where was he going? Where could anyone go on the beach at this hour?

She watched him start from the room. He hesitated and returned to the dresser. Holding his breath, he opened her purse. His fingers closed over the flat fold of bills inside it. He let the purse close, snapped it, and turned around.

Bernice sat up in the bed.

"Ah, my lobster creole," he said. He shoved his hand into his trousers pocket and brought it out empty.

"Where are you going?"

"I—I was hungry. Thought I'd go out for something to eat."

"Where will you find anything to eat this time of the morning?"

His eyes met hers. "Oh, I'll find some place. You want to go along?"

"No. I don't feel like it. Not this morning."

She meant she really wanted him to beg her to go. That would save them. That would make everything all right. Just to be wanted.

He didn't even argue with her, though.

As he passed her bed, he bent over and touched his lips to her fevered forehead.

"When you come back," she said, "bring a new bottle of lotion. My whole body is burning up."

"O.K. You want me to call the doctor for you?"

"Yes. Please."

He stood in the doorway for a moment looking at her.

Something was wrong. Terribly wrong. The wrong screamed in the room.

"Take it easy, baby," he said. The way he said it frightened her. It was a farewell the way he said it.

She opened her mouth to call after him, and then didn't. To want was one thing—that was hell. To be wanted—that was all that mattered. Her eyes filled with tears. Without that, you had nothing.

She willed him to turn around and ask her again to go with him. Just to coax her a little. But he didn't look back. He went out the cottage door and left it ajar. Bernice sank back on the damp sheets of her bed.

She couldn't stay there. It wasn't the painful burning of her flesh that brought her off the bed. Carlos was leaving. She pushed herself up on her elbows and tried to find Carlos through the bedroom window. There was no one in the shell roadway between the motel cottages. She got up and went over to the window.

She could see him then. He was standing up on the edge of the highway, tall and handsome as a god. Well, the girls on Olympus had had no picnic if all the handsome gods had been like Carlos. She looked at him, at the wide shoulders, the blond hair glistening in the early-morning sunlight. He appeared godlike. But he was much less than that in bed.

She sighed. That was the trouble between them, her passion annihilated him. She wanted him so terribly that looking at him stirred her. And when she was in his arms, she could never get enough of him. He hated to go to bed with her now. And she knew why. It angered him to know that when he did go to bed with her, he was going to leave her moaning and weeping in the agony of frustrated desire. It made him hate her. She could see it. And worse than that, it made him hate himself.

In a sudden feeling of compassion and tenderness for him, Bernice wanted to call out to him to wait for her. She would make herself over. She would be what he wanted. If only he would let her go with him. That was all she asked. She stood there at the window and silently begged him to come back and get her.

Through her tears, Bernice saw Carlos step out on the

highway and flag the Clearwater bus. Her heart lurched. Why? Where was he going? Why to Clearwater? And why hadn't he told her? Why had his voice sounded so final when he'd said, "Take it easy, baby"?

The bus stopped. The bottomless voices wailed inside Bernice. She began to feel dizzy. He wasn't ever coming back. He was leaving her and he wasn't ever coming back. She wanted to run screaming out into the court after him.

He got in the bus. There were only a few riders at this hour, mostly domestics and yardmen on their way to work.

The flesh across her shoulders seemed to shrivel. The heat was intense. And under the layer of fire she was cold and she began to shiver. She looked at the broken jar beside the bed. There was no lotion for her burns. Carlos hadn't even got any lotion for her. He didn't even give a damn.

When the bus was gone, gray exhaust trailing out behind it, Bernice went back across the room and sat on the bed. Carlos was leaving her. He wasn't coming back. She knew. Maybe it was the set of his shoulders as he boarded the bus. The way he hadn't looked toward the cottage again. Everything was so final. He wasn't coming back.

She lay on the bed and tried to sleep. But she couldn't. The pain in her blistered skin was intolerable. She had to lie still to stand it at all. Her loneliness made her twist and turn on the rumpled sheets. She needed something that would make her sleep. Something that would make her sleep for a long time. The kind of stuff that would expel every memory of Lloyd Deerman. Because she wanted to sleep to escape the thought that Carlos was leaving her. But she was afraid to sleep. Lloyd Deerman lived in her nightmares.

She got up and called the doctor. While she waited for him, she found a shoulderless sun dress. Painfully she pulled it on. By the time she was in it, she was sweating. She was tired but she looked at the bed and knew she couldn't rest. How could she rest? When her mind was quiet, Lloyd stalked into it and stumbled and fell down the steep endless stairs. And she told herself she could even have stood that. She was willing to pay the price if only she got what she wanted. But that was it. She had nothing she wanted!

Oh, she'd got away with murder, and she had Lloyd's hidden money. But she had walked into hell: the hell of frustration. The kind of frustration that drove you insane. You knew what you wanted, you had it right with you, but it was rotten in the middle. It was no good. It was desire and excitement and sweet agony and it was always frustrated.

The doctor knocked at the door. She told him to come in. She watched the twist of his mouth when he found the broken lotion bottle. His eyes said he knew what had happened, and she saw what he thought of her for letting it happen. To hell with him. There was no time she wouldn't want Carlos. There was always the thought that sometime it was going to be right for them. Sunstroke wouldn't matter then. Nothing would matter.

Only when, God? When?

The doctor spread lotion on her burns and went away. She looked at the clock on the table beside her rumpled bed. It wasn't time for the restaurant to open. She couldn't have breakfast yet. Not here on the beach. She remembered the dress shop owned by Elhanner. Maybe if she could buy a few dresses, some underthings, it might take her mind off Carlos. It would help her forget for a little while. Her back was cooler now, and she decided it was unreasonable to think Carlos wasn't coming back. She had to stop being a neurotic wife.

She got more money from her hiding place and went out of the cottage, closing the door after her. When she came back, Carlos would be there. He would raise hell because she had spent more money on herself. Everything would be lovely then. Oh, God, let him be here!

Elhanner's shop was open. He smiled at her. "My goodness," he lisped. "You'll just have to take it easier, dearie. That old sun has simply cooked you."

Bernice nodded. "Have you any dresses that will set off my new look?"

Where are you, Carlos?

"Goodness, no. I think you're wrong to buy anything until your skin darkens. You know, you'll very likely peel. You certainly won't be very pretty then."

"Show me some dresses anyhow. What does the well-boiled lobster wear down here this season?"

Without enthusiasm, Elhanner brought out his latest beach creations. Bernice couldn't get Carlos out of her mind. She looked at the dresses. She tried to concentrate on them. She spent two hours in the shop. When she finally left, she had bought only half a dozen underthings.

The restaurant was open now. She looked at the menu. She wasn't hungry. She went instead to Dugan's bar. There were no customers in the small green-tinted room. Dugan was polishing glasses. He looked up as she came in the door.

"Done to a turn," he said. "You're done to a turn."

"Give me a whisky sour."

"Right."

"Carlos said I owe you some money."

"Right." He consulted a tab beside his register. "Ninety bucks."

"Ninety dollars! What for?"

"Dog racing, honey. They run dogs down at Sarasota. But they don't run the right ones for your Carlos."

"You take bets here?"

"I'm not supposed to. But I do. They know about it. Costs me a kick-in. What the hell? I can afford it. I got Carlos. You and me both got Carlos." He slid the whisky sour across the bar. "He's gone, has he?"

She looked up. "Why?"

"Oh, I saw him leave on the bus this morning. Is he coming back?"

She stared at him. "Of course!"

"Is he? Those punks are cut pretty much to a pattern, Bernice. If he comes back this time, he'll leave you later. Sooner or later. You'd be lucky if it was sooner."

"He's not going to leave me. He'll never leave me."

She finished the drink and slid off the stool. "I was going to stay in here and drink. But you talk too much."

She took her packages and went out on the green sidewalk. She walked toward the restaurant. Damn Dugan. He had expressed her own thoughts. Carlos was leaving her. Damn him. Dugan had no right to know. Did he have to know everything?

She entered the restaurant. She almost laughed aloud. There was Carlos at a table, eating breakfast. The sickness in her stomach slid out as though it had never been there.

Carlos looked up, cheeks distended with food. The little blonde waitress was standing at his side talking to him. Carlos chewed, watching Bernice come toward him. He swallowed, his face flushing with the effort. He smiled at her.

What a hell of a smile!

"Thought you were sick in bed."

The waitress turned, smirking at the film of ointment spread all over Bernice's blistered body. For a moment their eyes clashed.

Bernice looked at Carlos. He was again bolting his food. He hadn't even asked her to sit down.

She opened her mouth to speak, and then didn't. She watched his handsome head bent wolfishly over his French toast. Fascinated, she stared. That wasn't hunger. That was greediness. What she had thought so sweet and dear when she'd first known him she now recognized as gluttony. He ate as though he could never get enough—as though he coveted everything in the world and more.

Bernice turned and retraced her steps across the café.

Dugan looked up when she re-entered his bar. He wasn't smiling.

"He's back, eh?"

"He's back. I want another drink."

"Sure. What you want this time?"

"How do I know? I don't know anything about liquor. You fix something."

He nodded. "My first wife ran off and left me. The guy she lammed with looked like your husband. Like they were twins. She took me for everything I had, and this guy spent it. That was a long time ago. The guy is probably forty by now. Looks like hell. He couldn't even satisfy her after he got her. He couldn't spend her money fast enough. Boy, she went through hell. Came back, wanted me to take her back."

Bernice looked at him. "Did you?"

He nodded. "Sure. But that don't make me like pretty boys like your husband any better." He pushed a drink toward her. "Here, try this. A clear alcoholic mind is what you need."

"That's what I need."

"Sure you do."

He was lining odd-shaped glasses on the bar before her. "Drink these as I mix 'em. You'll have it."

"I thought mixing drinks was dangerous."

"Don't you trust me?"

"Sure. Why not?"

She picked up the first small glass. She held her breath and drained it off. With the second one she forgot to hold her breath, and the fourth she sipped slowly, and didn't even feel the burn of it.

Chapter Twelve

Vaguely Bernice remembered that Carlos found her in the bar and took her home. It still puzzled her why Carlos had left her this morning and returned as he had. With her clear alcoholic mind she saw surely that Carlos had meant to leave her forever. And yet he was back. He was helping her out of Dugan's bar, and Dugan was watching them, and Bernice knew the expression that was on Dugan's face, even without being able to see Dugan at all.

She didn't speak to Carlos as they passed the stores in the modernistic green building. She was silent and paced with the grave dignity of the exceedingly drunk past the crowded shuffleboard courts.

At their cottage she shrugged free of his arms and walked ahead of him. The step skidded away from her and she would have fallen, but Carlos leaped forward and caught her. She looked at him but didn't bother to thank him.

Inside the door, she began to undress. She was aware that Carlos was talking. His voice was passionate and insistent and, she felt, disapproving. She slid the strapless dress down over her hips and dropped it on the floor. She stepped out of her shoes, staggered into the bedroom, and fell across her bed.

She sensed that Carlos had sat down on the edge of the bed and that he was undressing.

She was assailed by extreme sadness. It already seemed a hundred years ago since the very sight of Carlos' bare body had thrilled her, numbed her, and left her speechless with delight. Everything was a hundred years ago. It had been at least that long ago since it had been a thing of beauty to watch Carlos wolf down a meal.

He was still talking. The room spun about her head, and she could hear the cars on the highway, and somebody's radio was too loud, and she could hear the laughter from the shuffleboard court. But she couldn't understand what Carlos was saying. Only his tone of disapproval got through to her. How dare he disapprove of her! Her breath came fast and angry. She sat up on the bed with the room spinning around her and stared at him.

"Shut up!" she said. "You shut up! Suppose I had a drink. You stole it. You stole that money right out of my purse. You thief! Shut up. You fool. You didn't even have to. You could have had anything just by asking. But you stole it. Oh, you fool. You stole it!"

That was a long and tiring speech. She sagged backward on the bed.

She felt Carlos' hands on her and she shook them away.

She struggled to speak again. "Oh, no, you stole it. You stole it and you didn't have to. And now you can't ever have anything. Because I'm free of you. All I got to do is drink enough and I'm free of you. Oh, no."

"You don't mean that."

"I never meant anything more."

His hands were moving over her. She tried to twist away, out of his reach, but suddenly she couldn't force herself to go away from him. She reached up, pulling him down on her. Her heart thudded under his. And she thought, What a fool I am. How helpless I am against him.

The last thing she remembered before she fell asleep was the look on Carlos' face. A look of contempt.

He knows, too. He knows I haven't a defense in the world against him.

She woke up with a splitting headache at eleven A.M.

She staggered into the bathroom, took a cold shower, and dressed. When she came out into the front room, Carlos was there.

She looked at him, astonished. Her voice was bitter. "What's the matter, is it raining outside?"

95

"Why?"

"You wouldn't be in here if it weren't."

She knew how bitter her voice was but she couldn't help it. She looked at Carlos. He had never looked handsomer or fresher or younger. Oh, God, how she loved him! How she needed him!

"I'm sorry about the money, Bernice. I didn't mean to steal it. I thought you were asleep. I was going out to eat. I was broke. I didn't think you'd mind."

"I didn't mind, until I saw you get on the bus for Clearwater."

I don't care what you do, only don't leave me, Carlos. Don't leave me.

"I was just running into town."

"No."

"What the hell you think?"

"You were leaving me."

"I wasn't."

"Yes, you were. You took that money. And you were leaving me. Why?"

"I only rode into Clearwater. Why would I want to leave you?"

"Why don't you tell me?" Oh, God, tell me you love me. But she couldn't stop that shrewish voice. "I knew. You were running away."

He shrugged. "All right. We can't get along. I thought I might as well."

"So now at least you're telling the truth. Maybe you'll tell me why you came back!"

"I tried to leave. And I couldn't. I decided, Bernice. Things will be better. I swear it."

"You're lying again."

"I'm back, aren't I?"

"Yes. But why?"

He got up and put his arms around her. He smiled, pulling her close so her body fitted against his. Perfect, Bernice thought. As though we were really made for each other. But she knew Carlos wasn't thinking that at all. He knew every trick there was to know, and this was one of them. "Forgive me, baby. I'll be a good boy," he said.

She tried to twist away, but she couldn't.

"You won't be good. You're a liar and I know that now."

"I'm what you want."

She struggled, again. "You won't be. I won't let you."

"Doesn't it feel good like this, Bernice?"

"No. Let me alone."

"See, Bernice, so nice. So nice. You want me back, don't you, Bernice?"

"Yes. All right. I do. My God, I can't help that. I love you. That's why I'm here."

A smile twisted his face and he stepped away from her. For a moment she wavered and almost fell.

"O.K., Bernice. Maybe you're right. We don't get along. I'll clear out. This time I'll really go."

But Bernice was thinking about the feel of his body against hers, the need of her body for his. The awful need. The sick need.

"No, Carlos."

"Sure. You don't want me. Isn't that what you said? I'm a liar. I stole from you. Why'd you want me around?"

"Carlos, stop. You're torturing me."

"O.K. So if I get out I won't torture you."

"All right. You've twisted it around until I'm begging you. I'm begging you, Carlos. What do you want? What do you want?"

He took a step forward. His crafty eyes went over her face. "You want me back, eh?"

"Please don't leave me."

"I couldn't stay here unless I was happy, could I?"

"All right, Carlos. What do you want?"

"I'm tired of having to tell Dugan you'll pay him. That hurts a guy, having people look at you the way Dugan does. You can either shell out a hundred a day or I'm not staying. Good God, Bernice, the way you treat me, it makes a man sick."

"All right, Carlos."

"If I had a car I could get around. I wouldn't have to go in that bar. The dogs are running in Sarasota. I could get over there."

"But look, Carlos, you're just wasting money on the dogs. You don't ever win. You can't win."

"O.K. I'll get out. I told you I would. I won't be treated

97

like some goddamn lap dog. I ain't no goddamn lap dog, Bernice. I can't sit around doing nothing. I got to be doing what I want to do, or I go nuts."

"Will you love me, Carlos?"

"Sure. I told you I would, didn't I? You'd like to go to bed right now, wouldn't you? That makes it swell. Only we do it my way. From now on, everything is my way."

And she knew it all had changed. Once the intensity of her passion had been enough. She had been able to get Carlos when she wanted him. But Carlos had changed that. It was on a different basis now. His basis. Cash and carry.

Carlos paced up and down in the Tampa Cadillac agency office. There was a light in his face that Bernice had never seen before. He was like a kid at Christmas. He was getting just what he wanted. She looked at him. Maybe he'll be grateful. He'll know I love him. Things will be different.

She paid four thousand dollars cash for the blue convertible. Carlos insisted on waiting in the showrooms until the car was delivered. She wanted to see a movie while they serviced the new car. Carlos didn't even hear her. "We'll just wait right here. They promised me they could hurry it up."

He went through all the Cadillac display books. He was sweating and nervous. The more excited he became, the less aware he was of her.

It was nearly dark when they got back to the Rockledge Motel on the beach. Carlos said almost nothing on the drive back across Campbell Parkway from Tampa.

The lights in the green community center were bright.

"I'm hungry, Carlos. Why don't we eat dinner now?"

He pulled in to the curb before the restaurant. "Why don't you go ahead and eat, Bernice? I'll just drive up the road a little. I'm not hungry. God, how I love the way this thing runs!"

Bernice didn't want to get out of the car. She didn't want to leave Carlos. Didn't he understand that she tried to please him only because she wanted to keep him with her? Didn't he know that was why she had bought him the Cadillac?

She knew she couldn't let him see how frightened she

was, how dependent she was. She forced her mouth to move into an acid smile. She was the old Bernice now, talking sharp to keep from showing the hurt and the fear inside. She slid out of the car and slammed the door behind her.

"Be careful. Don't get any dust on it."

"If I do, I'll lick it off."

She watched him pull away from the curb and swing in a wide arc on the road. The pebbles flew from beneath the rear wheels. How perfect he looked in the smart new car! How they were made for each other!

She was no longer hungry. She looked at the bar and decided against it. She couldn't go on blanking out every night. After a while it wouldn't work any more. Then what?

She entered the restaurant. There were only a few people eating and Bernice crossed to the booth she and Carlos always used. It wasn't going to please her to have to eat under the cynical eyes of Carlos' little blonde waitress.

She looked up. The waitress was a dark-haired girl who didn't usually serve the booths.

The girl smiled. "Bet you were expecting Cookie."

"Who?"

"Cookie Dawson. The blonde kid. She usually waits on you. You and your husband."

"Oh? Yes. She isn't here?"

"No. She ain't. Tonight's her night off."

Bernice tried to eat. She ordered fried shrimp with cole slaw, tartar sauce, and French-fried potatoes. The shrimp were golden, standing up and pointing at her from the plate. It was the specialty of this restaurant. But for Bernice they were tasteless. She paid her check and left the restaurant.

On the sidewalk she realized she had nowhere to go. Carlos was still gone in the car. God knew when Carlos would return. She thought of the cottage, lonely and dark, the dreams waiting for her in the darkness of her bedroom. Lloyd would be falling and the splintering of the railings would scream in her ears.

She stood taut, her shoulders stiff and straight. She began to hear the juke-box music from Dugan's bar.

Suddenly she laughed, pleased with herself.

Dugan's was crowded at this hour. Women in brief beach-wear and men in sandals, shorts, and gaudy sport shirts sat at the tables and lined the bar. There were only two empty stools. Bernice sat on one of them.

Dugan smiled at her. "Again? So soon?"

"Yes."

He polished the bar before her. "Maybe you'd like a table?"

"No. I like it here. I'm lonely. I want somebody to talk to. If I sit at a table, I'll talk to myself."

"That'd never do. Probably a state law prohibiting it. What'll it be?"

"Where'd I leave off last night?"

"You want to start there?"

"I haven't been happier in years."

He fixed her a whisky sour. "That's the trouble with peo-ple," he told her as she drank. "They're always looking for happiness. Or something they think'll bring 'em happi-ness. That's why people are so miserable. If they'd just quit trying to be happy and relax and admit things are gone to hell, they wouldn't have to drink my liquor. I could close up, sit on the beach all day, and develop a pot gut."

"Another drink," Bernice said.

"There are a lot of things quicker," Dugan said. He shoved another drink at her. "This is the slow way, lady. It may take you years this way."

"The quick ways, they're against the law."

She looked at him. His eyes were on hers. She shivered. It was as though they were alone in the room.

Dugan's voice was very soft. "But sometimes it gets pretty rugged, eh? Looks like it's going to get worse, and looks like you can't stand it, eh?"

"Yes. Yes. That's it."

He polished the bar again, swiftly, putting a lot of pres-sure behind it.

"There are quicker ways than that stuff."

Bernice tried to laugh with him. She couldn't. What was there to laugh about? Carlos and her in their bed? Carlos and his new car? The splintering sound of ripping stair rails? The nightmares? The loneliness?

100

Dugan swiped at the bar again. "You know the right people," he said, "you can get anything you want."

Someone called Dugan and he moved away down the bar. Bernice watched him. In a moment he returned, held out a glass to her. It was brimming. She smiled eagerly, reaching for it.

Dugan held the drink just beyond the tips of her trembling fingers. "Sometimes you latch onto something that's too big for you," he said. "You got a rat in the house, you got to have rat poison, don't you? You got to know where to get it."

She stretched out her arm, closed her fingers around the drink. Their eyes met again.

"Anything you want," he told her, "I can get it for you."

Chapter Thirteen

Bernice was sick all the next day. This time she had no memory of how she got home. She slept until four in the afternoon. Her sleep was uninterrupted by nightmares, but when she woke she was alone and frightened, and haunted. How had she got home? Had there really been some man sitting on the stool beside her? Some man who laughed too loudly at everything she said? I'll see you home. Gee, you're awfully nice. I'm a nice guy. Only with you it's a pleasure, baby. Yes, I live right here. Maybe we better be quieter, we might wake up your husband. Wake up my husband? You'll have to yell pretty loud. He's in the next county. Gee, it was nice of you to see me home like this.

Bernice began to sweat. Wasn't that just a dream? And the way she hurled her body against his in the darkness? That was what she wanted with Carlos. That was all. Because if it had been real, maybe the man could have satisfied her. But in her dream, it had been just as terrible afterward as it had been with Carlos. Only worse. Because in this dream it hadn't been Carlos. She twisted, sweating on the bed.

She sat up, looking around. There was no sign that

anyone had been here with her. The bed was rumpled, but when she was finally asleep she was always restless, and the bed was always rumpled. It proved nothing.

Trembling, she got up and stared at her wan reflection. So that was what could happen to you when you blanked out. That could happen to you, and you'd never know for sure. You might meet a man on the street, and he would smile at you, and know he'd been in your bed. And you wouldn't know. He was just a stranger. Just a man you passed in the street.

She shuddered. She wasn't going to drink herself blotto like that any more. She thrust out her coated tongue and regarded it in the mirror. What had Dugan said? This was the slow way. The slow way to what? She felt a chill at the nape of her neck. The slow way to die.

She tried to repair the ravages of sleep in her face. But as she worked with the cosmetics she was thinking about Dugan. The bartender. The talkative bartender. A strange little man. Seeming to know what was inside her mind. He had looked at her and had known she was afraid of trying to live alone but didn't know how to die quickly. See me, Dugan had said meaningly. Anything you want, I can get it for you.

Well, she would stay away from that bar. Dugan gave her the creeps. Besides, even if she and Carlos weren't getting along well, it was her business. It didn't concern a strange little man named Dugan.

She went forlornly about the small cottage. There was no sign to show when Carlos had last been here. She dreaded the hours ahead without Carlos. It was more than the awful need for him. There were only two things that could keep her from thinking about Lloyd and remembering the way he'd died. Carlos was one. When she was with him, she was free of her dreams. The only other thing that could save her was drinking at Dugan's bar. What a lovely life she'd bought for herself!

When she was with Carlos, she was left tormented and raving with frustrated need. And worse than that, he had twisted their relationship around until he used her desire for him as a way to bleed her of money. It was cash and carry. Carlos knew what she wanted, and he made her pay for it.

102

That left only the drinks that Dugan prepared for her. And that led to what? The man's voice, the man's laughter, the indistinct gray of the man's face. I'll see you home. Gee, you're nice. I'm a nice guy, only with you it's a pleasure, baby.

She looked at her hands. They were shaking. She clenched her fists.

The doorbell rang. She stood in the center of the room and stared at the closed front door. Maybe it was the man from last night. If there had really been a man last night. She didn't even know. She only knew she didn't want to find out. The doorbell rang again, clattering and screeching against her raw nerves.

She padded across the gray rug of the living room. The doorbell rang again before she reached the front window and wailed at her again as she peered through the curtains. The breath sighed out of her.

She had never seen this man before, not even in her nightmares. The man at her front door was heavy-set. He was wearing a brown suit that was somehow gaudy and expensive-looking at the same time. His thick-jowled face was red and moist. Bernice saw that he had small blue eyes. There was anger in them as he punched at the doorbell. His thick mouth was firm. Bernice saw that he had no intention of going away. He intended to keep ringing the bell until someone answered him.

She opened the door. For a moment they looked at each other. The red-faced man took a monogrammed handkerchief from his pocket and mopped his forehead.

"Carlos Brandon live here?"

Bernice felt a tremor about her heart. Was it always to be like this, every time someone came to the door? Expecting the worst, afraid for Carlos, afraid to ask and afraid not to know?

"Yes. I'm his wife."

"His wife?" This seemed to please the big man. "May I come in, Mrs. Brandon?"

He'd already opened the screen door and was pushing by her into the living room. Purposefully, she waited until he was in the center of the room, then she said, "Yes. Come in. Please do."

She might as well have forgotten the irony. It was lost on the visitor.

There was a brief silence as the big man peered into the kitchenette, into the disordered bedroom, and through the opened door into the bath.

"Small," Bernice said. "But adequate."

"Looks nice, Mrs. Brandon. Looks real nice. Hope you like it down here. Hope you like it a lot."

"Are you a real-estate man? Or a greeter from the Chamber of Commerce?"

"Not me, Mrs. Brandon. I just came down from New York. Just flew into Tampa this morning. Came all the way to see Carlos. He's not around, you say?"

"No, he isn't."

"Couple of my boys saw him in Clearwater yesterday morning. Early. He grabbed a bus right back out here. My boys let him go. We knew where he was. That's all that mattered."

Bernice was weak. This dangerous man was telling her that he had been searching for Carlos. She found herself remembering the cue-dust-white man called Mitch, and the fright in Carlos' face. Mitch must have worked for this man. And he had run away from New York to escape them. Now they had found him down here. And worse than that, Bernice knew another truth. Carlos *had* been running away from her yesterday morning! But he had seen this man's hired killers in Clearwater. That was why he had come back!

She forced herself to speak. "I don't know when he'll be back."

"I'm in no hurry. I can wait."

"Are you a friend of his?"

"In a way. I was like a father to him. He done me some dirt, Mrs. Brandon. I may as well tell you that right off. My name is Bert Chester."

She shook her head. The name meant nothing. "I don't believe I've heard him mention you."

"No. I guess he wouldn't. I own a club up home. Club Holiday. Drinking. Dancing. Gambling. Ever hear of it?"

"No."

"No. I guess you wouldn't. But believe me, your husband knew about it. I used to try to keep him out. He was nuts about gambling and he wasn't heeled for it. I didn't want his business. He was always gettin' in over his head and going on the cuff. Most always I managed to collect. But I don't like that class of trade. Never did. Still don't. Bartenders and gamblers size up a man pretty quick, Mrs. Brandon. Your husband measured up to a punk. Just made it. A punk spending money as though he had it. If I sound burned about it, Mrs. Brandon, I am burned. I use my boys' time collecting his debts. He got into me for a sizable amount. Then he ran out. Naturally, I had to put a tracer on him. That's mighty easy in the syndicate. Especially on a man like Carlos Brandon, who can't stay away from gambling. When I found out where he was, I came down to collect. And that's what I'll do."

"He never mentioned that he owed you money."

"No. Why should he? You'll find, Mrs. Brandon, that he ain't the type to tell you much about himself. I bet he never told you about a widow named Vivian Barrows, did he?"

"No."

Bert Chester laughed. "She was a dopey widow, out to be young with Carlos. Well, he took her for plenty. Until she wised up and hired a private eye to follow him. Then she threw him out, burned everything he owned, and tossed him on his ear. I picked him up and helped him because he owed me money. I got him in at the Citizen's Bank. When he ran out on that job, he left me on the spot."

"You? What did you have to do with the bank?"

He laughed. "Nothing, baby. But I knew a few people who did. It wasn't hard to get your husband a minor job at the bank. He was in there where I wanted him. He was working for me to square that debt. He ran out."

"No. We got married. We came down here. On—our honeymoon."

"Yeah. I know all about it." Bert Chester looked at her. "That's one reason I came to talk to you. Thought it might help to talk to you first. Wanted to find out what the punk means to you. That's why I told you about Vivian Barrows. I wanted you to know that he's a two-timer. He's made a career out of living on women who'll take care of him. He's a welcher. Ran out owing me money. I got him a job and he ran out on that. He's a liar and a cheat and a fake. I tried to warn him not to run. I talked to him like a father. But he ran away. So that means he's a fool as well as a four-flusher. Now I'm giving you a break, Mrs. Brandon. I've told you what I know about Carlos Brandon. I've leveled with you. You know what he is. If you want to, you can pack a bag, I'll drive you to Clearwater. You can take a train anywhere you like. You won't ever need to hear about him again. You won't ever need to worry about him again."

Bernice stared at him. "What will happen to him?"

"You heard what I been telling you about him?"

"I heard you. What are you going to do to him?"

"You know the truth about him, and you still care what happens to him?" Bert Chester shook his head. "It don't make sense, sister. It just don't make sense."

Bernice met his eyes. "I can't help it. I love him. I couldn't just walk out and leave him."

"He could walk out and leave you, baby. Just give him time and that's what he'll do."

"Probably he will."

Bert Chester cursed. "I'd like to know what it is that attracts women to punks like this guy, makes 'em spend their lives taking care of 'em, gettin' 'em out of scrapes so they can get in worse ones next time. All right. So now we can talk. You're the only person who cares enough about Carlos Brandon to save him. I'm willing to let you."

She exhaled slowly.

"One thing you got to do. Keep him down here. Tell him I said so. Tell him he never got away from me. Tell him we could have moved in on him sooner. Tell him the string's run out with me. Keep him out of my way. If he ever comes back into any of my clubs, if I ever hear of him gambling in a place of mine—that's all. That's all for him."

"I'll do it. I promise you I'll do it."

"All right. Now there's one more thing. He owes me three thousand dollars. Vivian Barrows agreed to pay it. But she kept delayin' sendin' me a check until the bust-up came between them. Then she called me and said she wasn't going to pay his debts. She probably thought I'd have him killed and she wanted that, she wanted to be even with him for two-timing her. But I'm interested in money, and my rep. What I want is three grand. You pay me the three grand and Carlos is all yours. All yours."

"How will I know? You hate him. How do I know you won't kill him after you have your money?"

Bert Chester didn't smile. "Let's trust each other, sister. You got enough to worry about with Carlos. My word. You'll have to take my word for it."

"Just a minute."

She went into the bedroom, closed the door behind her.

Bert Chester looked at the uncomfortable chairs in the front room and decided to go on standing. He wanted a drink, but there was no liquor in the room.

The bedroom door opened and Bernice appeared. She had a stack of green bills clutched in her hand.

Bert Chester laughed. "Cash?"

"Yes. Do you mind?"

"No. This'll save clearing a check through a bank."

She counted out the money into his hand. He bent the stack, folded it, and shoved it into his coat pocket.

"Do I get a receipt?" Bernice said.

He handed her the I.O.U. Carlos had signed in the Club Holiday.

"Carlos is your receipt, baby." He looked at her a moment and then went to the front door. His hand on the knob, he turned and looked at her. "I've seen some suckers in my time, sister. But God help me, you're the damnedest sucker I ever met." The door slammed.

Bernice met her eyes in the living-room mirror. Well, she had made one more payment. And then she added, her mouth twisting, "Sucker."

Chapter Fourteen

It was almost dark when Carlos slid to a stop before his cottage, showering gravel from beneath his rear tires.

He slid out of the car, wadded a used Kleenex, and tossed it into the road. He whistled softly to himself as he went around the car and into the cottage.

Bernice was standing in the center of the darkened front

room. He caught his breath. Then he laughed and snapped on the light.

"Ah, the wrath of God. What's the matter?"

"Nothing. Why should anything be the matter? I love being cooped up here all day by myself. Did you have a good time?"

"Swell." He was thinking, I don't care what's eating you, baby. I just don't want to hear about it.

"You had company."

He hesitated, going tense. "That so? Who was it?"

She came to him and put her hands on his arms. "Do you love me, Carlos? Do you love me?"

"Sure. Look at me. I'm all goose pimples, baby. Tell me, who was here?"

"I hope you love me, Carlos."

"All right! I said I loved you. Who was here?"

"Because you cost me a lot of money."

Now his breath quickened and he felt the bottom drop out of his belly. He forced his voice to remain casual. "Do I? So what? You've got plenty of it."

"That's it, Carlos. I don't. We can't go on like this. And I haven't anything for you unless you love me."

He caught her hands in one of his and pulled them down, pressing back on her fingers.

"I said, who was here?"

"Bert Chester."

"What did he say?"

"You're hurting me."

"When will he be back?" His gaze flew around the room. "He's not here now?"

"No. He's gone."

"We've got to get out of here, Bernice. Now. Tonight."

"Why?"

"He's going to kill me."

"Why would he want to kill you?"

His voice hardened. "Oh, something he thinks I did. He tried to give me a hard time in New York. But I told him off. I told him to stay away from me."

"He says you owe him three thousand dollars."

"All right! If you know what he wanted, why did you ask me?"

"I just wondered if you could ever stop lying."

"So now you know. What did Chester say?"

"He said to tell you to stay down here. He said if he ever saw you again he'd kill you."

"What about the three thousand dollars? What did he say about that?"

"I paid it."

"That ends it?"

"He said it did. If you stayed down here."

He breathed heavily through his open mouth. "Oh, God. What a hell of a thing. I tell you, I'm sorry you threw that money away like that."

"What?"

"Why, he was bluffing. You know he was. Gamblers can't collect, not crooks like Chester. Not if you've guts enough to fight 'em. Everything in that place of his is crooked."

"He says you knew that before you gambled. He said he never wanted you to gamble."

"He's just bluffing."

"He didn't look like a man who was bluffing."

"O.K.! So I'm scared to death."

"Yes. I think you are."

"All right. And so you saved my life."

"Yes. I did."

"So what do you want me to do now? Kiss your shoes? Promise to be a good little boy?"

"Yes. I do."

"Well, baby, it looks to me like you've been had. I never was afraid of Bert Chester. He's nothing but a hoodlum."

"Is that why you ran away from New York? Is that why you came running back from Clearwater? Oh, I thought it was because you loved me. But I know better now. You don't love anybody. You never could."

"We ran from New York because I thought we had something together. I'm not so sure now. You paying off on a gambling debt. Why didn't you tell him to wait? Why didn't you let me handle it? I never was afraid of him. You've been a sucker, baby."

"Yes, I know. I've already been told that."

He started by her toward the bedroom.

"Where are you going, Carlos?"

"Out."

She stood looking at him. She was remembering suddenly the anguish in Lloyd Deerman's voice the night he had died. She could see him asking Bernice where she had been. She remembered her curt answer, "I went out." When they don't love you, you can't make them love you. You can just hurt yourself, the way Lloyd had done. The way Bernice was hurting herself now.

She knew that now she had begun to think about Lloyd, she wasn't going to be able to get him out of her mind. She understood now the agony Lloyd had endured, loving her while she despised him. Seeing she was suffering as Lloyd had wasn't going to help her forget him. Poor blind devil. All he'd wanted was love and affection. She'd given it to him! She'd run at him, her arms like thin battering rams. He had fallen, twisting and rolling . . .

She knew she couldn't stand to be alone again, especially not tonight.

"Take me with you," she begged.

"Sorry, Bernice." He shrugged her hand off his arm. "Not this time."

"Don't go, then. Please don't leave me. Carlos, listen to me. Anything you want. Anything you want to do, Carlos. Please stay with me. Just tonight. Please don't go out again."

He stopped in the bedroom door and looked at her. "Sorry, baby. My plans are already made."

He watched the stiff way she walked across the room and sank down on the divan. She laid her head back and stared at the ceiling. Carlos shrugged. He went into the bathroom and started the shower. He was singing over the roar of the water. When he came out, Bernice was still sitting on the divan. She looked as though she hadn't moved a muscle.

He dressed carefully, admiring himself in the mirror, taking a lot of time so that he looked just right.

Bernice's purse was on the dresser. He opened it. There was only a ten-dollar bill in it. He grimaced as he shoved the money into his trousers pocket.

When he started through the living room, Bernice turned her head on the couch. "Please, Carlos."

"I've told you, baby, I'm sorry as hell. But that's the way it is."

He bent over to kiss her, but she turned her face away. His mouth tightened and he straightened up.

"Don't wait up for me," he said.

"Carlos."

He was at the front door. Immediately he glared across his shoulder.

"Carlos, what kind of life do we have? What kind of life is this, with you running around, and me sitting here?"

"Don't try to hold me, baby. I'm used to being free. I can't help it. That's the way I want it."

"What am I to do?"

"Look. Tomorrow night we'll plan something big. How about it? Tomorrow night?"

She didn't answer. He waited a moment and then he went out, letting the door slam. He heard her sob. One painful sob. And then it was silent in the bright little cottage. Oh, the hell with it, he told himself. She'd spoil every damned thing he wanted to do if he'd let her.

He slid into the car and started the engine. The smooth, powerful sound of it made him smile and he felt better.

He put the car in reverse and moved along the court. He could feel the eyes of the other tenants on him. The hell with them. Old goats with nothing to do but mind somebody else's business.

A car moved across the court exit. Carlos slammed on his brakes. There were only inches between his bumper and the fender of the other car. The other car. It was big, dark blue, mud-splattered. The car Carlos had seen in Clearwater. Mitch's car.

Carlos felt his stomach turn over. For a moment he thought he was going to puke.

Before he could move, Draper was standing at the door of his car. "Just let it sit, Carlos."

"It can't just sit here."

"Get out."

"Are you crazy? There are people around here. You can't get away with anything."

"Neither can you. Don't make me mad, Carlos. Do like I said. Turn off the engine. Leave the keys in it and get out. Do it now."

Carlos fumbled at the ignition. Draper opened the door

for him. When Carlos' feet touched the pavement, his knees caved in and he almost fell.

"Right over there. Right in the front seat, Carlos."

Mitch was behind the steering wheel. He looked at Carlos. He didn't bother smiling. "Hi, Carlos."

"Hi, Mitch." Carlos felt Draper crowd into the car beside him. He was pressed between Mitch and Draper. He began to sweat. Mitch put the car in gear and they sped along the darkened highway.

"Look, Mitch. We paid it. Bernice paid the three grand. Bert said that was all he wanted."

"That's right," Mitch said. "That's all he wanted. Wasn't that all he wanted, Draper?"

"Not exactly," Draper said.

"Oh, my God," Carlos whispered.

Draper was looking out the car window. "This looks all right."

"Nah," Mitch said. "I know a place four or five miles down the beach. More private."

"What you guys going to do?"

"Nothing, kid. You see, Bert has got his three grand. All he wants is to impress you a little."

"Look. I'm impressed."

Draper grunted. "He's scared as hell, all right. That's the truth."

"No," Mitch said. "He impresses too easy. He forgets too easy. This time you ain't going to forget, Carlos."

He swung the car left off the highway into a small dirt road that twisted through a grove of thick green matted bushes.

They came out on a bare stretch of ground. Mitch parked the car. Draper got out.

"O.K., punk," Draper said. "Get out."

"No."

"Don't be a damn fool. Get out!"

Mitch touched his arm. "Get out, kid."

Carlos was too weak to move. Draper caught his arm and dragged him off the seat. Carlos' knees banged on the running board and he sank to the ground.

Mitch came around the car. He caught Carlos' tie in his fist, twisting it. "Get up, Carlos."

As he twisted, Carlos' face turned red, and abruptly he could no longer breathe. Mitch began to lift on the tie, and Carlos stood up, stretching tall.

"That's better," Mitch said. He twisted the tie again. Carlos could feel his eyes bulge. His teeth ached all around his gums. It was as though the blood pressure were going to force them out of his head. Strangling, he tried to speak and flailed wildly with his arms.

"Stand still," Mitch said. He twisted the tie again, and when Carlos flung out his arms and jerked his head back trying to breathe, Mitch drove his knee into Carlos' groin.

As Carlos doubled over, Mitch drove his fist into Carlos' blood-swollen face. The blow hurt every inch of Carlos' head. It seemed to loosen his teeth, it seemed to drive his eyes from their sockets, and it sent the blood spewing into his ears, deafening him. It made him forget the agony of his scrotum.

He caved to his knees. But they wouldn't let him fall any farther. Mitch kept his hand twisted in that tie. Carlos' head was flopping as he tried to breathe. His lungs were afire and his heart had gone crazy, pounding in its need for oxygen.

Every time his head flopped they hit him in his face. He felt his nose break, and the blood spurted from his eyes. But he couldn't breathe any more, and without breathing, nothing else mattered. His head began to spin, and the pain was nothing beside his need to breathe, and then it was all darkness. He heard nothing and felt nothing and saw nothing. He was careening through a vacuum trying to get one breath of air.

Funny how you never knew how much breathing meant, until you couldn't breathe any more.

Chapter Fifteen

The telephone rang.

Bernice was still sitting on the divan where Carlos had left her. Her head was bent away from his kiss, and she was too tired to move. She had lain there, perfectly still, as the minutes dragged into hours, in an almost catatonic

113

trance: not resting, her muscles rigid, her mind completely numbed.

At first the ringing of the telephone came through to her from a long way off, as though the bell were in another cottage along the court. Finally the insistent clamor bored through her torpor and she straightened up on the couch.

She got up and moved across the room. The telephone began to shrill as she picked it up.

"Hello," Bernice said. She could hear a radio's muted tones in the background, but there was no answer. "Hello," she said again. She heard the connection being broken almost stealthily.

Bernice stood there with the receiver in her hand. She dropped it back on its cradle. If it rang again, she wouldn't answer it.

She went back to the couch. She picked up one of the magazines from an end table. She couldn't concentrate on the bright pictures. The stories seemed dull and unappealing.

The telephone began to wail again. Bernice smiled to herself and went on sitting there.

The doorbell clanged in the middle of the ringing of the telephone.

Pleased that there was something to do, something to end the long period of apathy and inertia, Bernice got up, lifted the receiver. "Hello?" When she heard the connection being cut off a second time, she replaced the telephone and went to the front door.

The court owner stood there. He smiled, but Bernice could see that it was an effort.

"Hello, Mrs. Brandon. How are you this evening?"

"I'm all right. Will you come in?"

"No. Not this time. A funny thing has happened. I've been waiting to see if he'd return. You see, I don't like to interfere with my people here in the courts. I don't want them to think that I'm an old busybody. I like to give the people who stay here complete freedom. Reason most people come to Florida, I figure, is to get away from the lives they've lived up home. So here at Rockledge, I say they can get away with anything they like in my cottages—short of murder, eh? Heh-heh. Anything short of murder."

"Yes. What is it? What has happened?"

The telephone began to clatter behind her. She stiffened against the sound of it.

"Your telephone, Mrs. Brandon. Answer it. I can wait."

"Let it ring. It must be a wrong number. I've answered it twice, and nothing happens."

"Yes, sometimes it does that," the motel owner agreed. But plainly the sound of the unanswered bell offended his orderly mind. "Well, Mr. Brandon went off and left your new car parked right in the entrance of the court. Some folks have just cut out around it, but others are complaining. I'm afraid somebody will swing in from the highway. Might be a lot of damage done."

Bernice looked beyond him. She could see the sleek car gleaming in the neon lights of the motel sign. She frowned. "I'll move it."

She went with the owner out along the roadway. She could hear the wail of the telephone, racing after her, reaching at her. She knew they were both conscious of it. She got in the car and drove it to her cottage. The telephone was still ringing.

Taking her time, Bernice removed the ignition keys and rolled up the car windows. She got a perverse pleasure from hearing the jangling of the telephone.

When she entered the cottage, she strode across the room and grabbed up the receiver.

"Hello," she said. "Who is this? What do you want?"

"Is Carlos there?" It was a guarded voice. A woman's voice.

"Who is this?" Bernice said. She felt suddenly feverish. She knew then how that widow, Vivian Barrows, must have felt when she found Carlos with another woman.

"Is Carlos there?" the voice said again.

"No. He isn't."

She heard the connection snapped off. Her hands trembling, Bernice stood with the receiver clutched in her fingers. She dialed the operator.

"I just had a telephone call," Bernice said. "Is there any way you could trace the call for me?"

"No, there isn't." The operator's voice was smug. "The connection has been broken. I'm sorry."

Bernice dropped the receiver. She looked about the room.

That woman's voice. The walls of the room seemed to be pressing in around her. Anger and jealousy made her weak and empty-bellied. She told herself she didn't care where Carlos was. She even hoped that Bert Chester had lied. She hoped that they had taken him out of the car. Maybe they had killed him. Why should he go on living? Such a rotten, lying tramp.

The tramp I love.

She felt the sting of hot tears. Crying. Crying for Carlos. Angered, she pulled off her glamour glasses and laid them on the table beside the telephone. She found a Kleenex and dabbed at her eyes. What a wonderful husband she had! He didn't want her, but any other woman would do. It wouldn't have been so bad if Carlos were simply a poor lover. A lot of men and a lot of women aren't vigorous sexually. She could have stood that. She loved him and she was content when he was with her. But he was an alley cat. She wondered if he went around leaving every woman as dissatisfied as she was.

She wandered into the bedroom and fell across the bed. Why had she murdered Lloyd Deerman? She stared at the ceiling. Because she had wanted to buy beauty and happiness. She wanted to be treated the way beautiful women were treated: the Rita Baehrs, and the lovely empty little bitches who traded simulated passion for advancement and homes and security and attention. And how sure she'd been that she had what she wanted that day when Carlos asked her to marry him and run away to Florida.

She could no longer stay on the bed. She couldn't stand the silence and the loneliness. There was just one thing to do. She would get dressed and go across the highway to Dugan's bar. She had no idea how long she could go on drinking herself into oblivion, waking up without knowing where she'd been. But for tonight, at least, it was the only answer.

She dragged out a powdery blue net dress she'd bought in Elhanner's shop.

The telephone rang. She dropped the dress in a heap and ran into the front room.

She grabbed up the telephone. "Hello. What do you want?"

"Is Carlos there?" the woman said. There was nothing guarded about her voice now.

"Who is this?" Bernice demanded.

"What difference does it make who it is? I want to talk to Carlos."

"I told you, he isn't here."

"Where is he?"

"I don't know."

"I think you're lying. If he's there, I want to talk to him. Tell him he'd better talk to me."

"He isn't here," Bernice replied.

"Where is he? I rode by. His car is there. I saw it. Tell him I want to talk to him."

Bernice laughed. "When he comes in, I'll tell him."

"You tell him now!"

Bernice laughed again. The frantic anxiety in the woman's voice pleased her. It changed everything. It made her master of this situation. She replaced the telephone.

Immediately it rang again.

Bernice picked it up. "Good night," she said. "Pleasant dreams."

She cut the connection and then placed the telephone off its hook on the table. She slipped on her glasses and started back to the bedroom. Carlos, it seemed, couldn't be true to anyone, except in his own inimitable way.

There was someone at the front door. Bernice paused, listening.

"Bernice!" It was Carlos' voice.

She ran across the room, pulled open the wooden door, and stared at Carlos, stretched across the front stoop.

She caught her breath, and for a moment didn't move. She had a strange thought in that flash of time. She'd once read a mystery short story called "The Monkey's Paw." She had never been able to get it out of her mind. In her imagination, she had been able to see the ruined body of the son as he struggled back to the front door of the cottage in answer to his mother's prayers and the magic of the monkey's paw. For that instant, Bernice thought she was seeing that gory apparition.

"Bernice," Carlos whispered. "Help me inside. For God's sake, help me inside."

Repelled at the sight of his bloody, torn face, Bernice helped Carlos in to the couch.

"I'll call a doctor," she said.

He caught her arm. "No. Don't do it."

"Your nose is broken. One of your eyelids is cut."

"I don't care. I don't want a doctor. I'll be all right. Just get something from the medicine chest. Get this stuff off my face. I'll be all right."

She looked down at him. "Why should I help you?"

"Please. Good God, Bernice, not now. I'm in agony."

"There are all kinds of agony, Carlos. I'm in agony, too."

"Please, Bernice, I came back to you. I just kept telling myself that when I got back to you, I'd be all right."

"And now you're not, are you?" she said. "If there's anything wrong with you, you'll have to fix yourself. I won't touch you. When you're through, you can get out."

"Bernice! My God, I can't walk. I can't move! I'm nearly dead. Haven't you any pity?"

"No. I haven't. Some woman has been calling you all evening. Why don't you go to her? Maybe she would pity you."

His head rolled loosely on the divan. "Oh, God, Bernice, I came to you."

"Yes," she said. "You always do when you need help, don't you?"

"This is different, Bernice. My God, can't you look at me and see that? I'm in trouble, Bernice. Bad. This time if you'll help me, if you'll take me back, I'll make it up to you. So help me God, Bernice. I'm through pretending I'm anything I'm not. I'm back to you on my knees. Help me, and I'll make it up to you. I'll be what you want, Bernice. So help me God."

For a long time she looked at him, the broken nose, the bleeding eyes staring at her, beseeching her. She walked over and dropped the telephone receiver back in its cradle. They both waited, without breathing. The silence stretched out, and they both exhaled heavily. Bernice turned around and looked at Carlos again.

"I'll get something," she said quietly. "I'll fix your face."

Chapter Sixteen

Lloyd was falling. Rolling, twisting, falling. His neck dangled crazily. His eyes, sightless, obscenely white, moved, followed her no matter how far he fell. . . .

Bernice awoke. She was cold, nauseated. She was certain she was going to be sick at her stomach, but she was afraid to get out of her bed in the darkness. The nightmare and the fear in the nightmare had taken her insides in clammy talons and twisted them dry. She lay flat on her back, trying to burrow deeper into the mattress. Her eyes were wide open now, staring up at the darkened ceiling.

She wondered what time it was, but knew she couldn't even reach out a chilled arm for the small bedside clock. She could only lie, tense and rigid, and pray that Carlos would come home soon.

She was too cold and too frightened for tears. Yet she wanted to cry. The whole thing had started all over again with Carlos. His smashed nose was not broken. His face healed quickly. As soon as he was well, Carlos seemed to forget what had happened to him. A week and a half he lay around the cottage, walked with her on the beach, lolled morose in the Cadillac while Bernice took him for long drives. He was attentive and almost kindly.

Bernice twisted on the bed. She had been content. She knew Carlos well enough so that she no longer asked anything of him. It was good to have him all to herself. There had been no dreams, no nagging, bottomless voices crying insistently after her. She had slept and wakened and eaten regularly.

She heard a car far off on the highway. She strained, listening to it as it came near and then sped past in the darkness. It had begun again last night. Carlos had walked out after dinner and returned just before dawn. The night had been hell. Bernice had tried not to sleep, and had fallen asleep fighting it. The dreams began at once, and the wailing, sobbing voices. In her dreams she ran swiftly, but not fast enough to escape Lloyd's white, sightless eyes. She turned on all the lights and was sitting up in the middle of the bed when Carlos came in.

The look he had hurled her dared her to find fault. But she was too relieved to have him with her to care where he had been. The next day she cared. The next morning she was ill with anger and jealousy. And tonight she'd sobbed herself to sleep, and wakened from a nightmare too horrible to endure.

She heard a car swing into the motel driveway. When she heard the sound of the braked wheels outside her window and knew it was Carlos, she relaxed and turned over on her side. He was whistling as he came in the front door. He slammed it behind him. She pretended to be asleep when he came in the bedroom.

So this is what my money has bought me. Not much. Nothing. Less than nothing.

At ten o'clock the next morning, Carlos was still snoring into his pillow. Quietly Bernice slid out of bed. She bathed and returned to the bedroom. She found that Carlos had taken all the money from her purse again last night before he went out.

She didn't want to touch the money she had hidden. Carlos might wake up. She couldn't ever let him find that money. It was the only hold she had on him at all now. She knew the truth as only the completely disillusioned ever know it. Carlos was not only greedy; he coveted everything. He hated the idea of anyone's having anything that might some way be his.

She went to the chair where he'd tossed his trousers when he came in. She found a five-dollar bill in the pocket. When she withdrew her hand, a small slip of white paper fluttered to the floor. She picked it up and unfolded it. It had been scribbled hastily, in pencil, a single letter and numbers: "C-75633."

She closed her fingers over the paper and the five-dollar bill. She put them both in her purse. Moving stealthily, she chose the most flattering dress she'd bought at Elhanner's, white piqué with flared shoulders and slash pockets.

She worked a long time on her face to the background

120

music of Carlos' uninterrupted snoring. When she was dressed, she looked down at Carlos and went into the front room. She closed the bedroom door behind her.

She sat on the edge of a chair at the end table. She took the slip of paper from her purse. She didn't need it. She had memorized the numbers on it. She lifted the receiver and dialed C-75633.

The telephone rang a long time. Her face set, Bernice sat stiffly on the edge of the chair, hearing the sound across the wires. Finally there was a rumble as though someone fumbled with the receiver and a woman's sleepy voice answered, "Hey-o?"

"Cookie?" Bernice said. Her heart was pounding.

"Yes." Cookie's voice lost its bedroom warmth when she found it was a woman she was talking to. "Who is this? What you want, middle of the night like this?"

"I want to talk to you," Bernice said. She listened for movement in the bedroom.

"Who is this?"

"Bernice Brandon."

"Oh." There was a brief charged silence. "What you want to talk to me about?"

"I think you know."

"And I don't think I do."

"I'm coming to see you, anyway. Where do you live? You may as well tell me. I'll find out from the restaurant."

"My, you are persistent, aren't you?"

Bernice laughed coldly. "You'll find there's nothing I won't do to have what I want."

"All right," Cookie said. Her voice was defiant. "I live at Gulf Sands. Apartment Eight-A. Come on over. You won't get anywhere with me. You're not the only one who knows what she wants. But I'm awake now. I think I can stand talking to you. I'll have some coffee first."

Bernice parked the Cadillac outside the Gulf Sands Apartments. A rambling, single-storied building of white stone, it was shining brightly in the sun. Bernice knew the place was expensive. It had that look. How did a waitress afford an apartment like this?

She slid out of the car and slammed the door after her. She had been cold and determined before. But now she

121

was angry. She'd found the front seat of the car covered with sand. It was all over the upholstery. Carlos and Cookie swimming in the moonlight. She remembered the way it had been, their bodies naked and lighted up with phosphorescence. Now it was Carlos and Cookie. Swimming together. Clinging together.

She was sick at her stomach. The things she wanted Carlos had. With some other woman.

What had she wanted all her life? To be treated as lovely women are treated; to be loved and wanted and noticed and made over. She shivered. She'd killed because that was what she wanted above everything else in the world. She was farther from her desire than ever.

At Apartment 8-A, she punched hard on the doorbell. Cookie Dawson answered at once. Her blonde hair was straggly and she'd tied an unbecoming negligee loosely about her waist. Bernice's spirits lifted a little. The waitress sported a round, protuberant little belly in unguarded moments like this.

Cookie dragged the back of her hand across her forehead to wipe away a stray wisp of hair. "Come on in."

The apartment was very small. The front room was eight by ten, divided from a kitchenette by a built-in bookcase that was a dish cabinet on its reverse side. The furniture was all new, impossibly uncomfortable stuff. The rooms were bright with fresh paint and there were Venetian blinds and frilly white curtains at the windows.

The front room was in disarray. Ash trays were overflowing. Glasses made rings on the tables. And more of that damned beach sand trailed across the rugs.

Cookie flopped on the divan and motioned Bernice to a chair. Bernice tried to take assurance from the fact that she was fashionably dressed, and that Cookie looked like a hangover. But she was aware that Cookie seemed perfectly at ease. There was even something more than faintly patronizing in her manner.

Bernice's hands were trembling. She sat awkwardly on one of the uncomfortable chairs. She could hear those old bottomless voices stirring inside her. Where was the role she had planned to play here this morning? The expensively attired wife talking down frankly to a cheap little waitress?

"You've been seeing my husband," Bernice blurted.

Cookie smiled at her. "Frequently."

"You've got to stop."

"Why?"

"He's my husband."

"I don't force him to come to see me. Do you force him to come to see me?"

"There are different kinds of force."

"And you're mad because you haven't got that kind, is that it?"

"If you're cheap enough, if you throw yourself at a man, I suppose you can make him notice you and want you, no matter what you are."

"Not if he's contented at home."

"No man is contented at home when some strange little bitch is throwing herself at him."

"Let's keep it friendly. You're getting hysterical."

"Why shouldn't I?"

"It won't help you any, that's why. You came over here to tell me that I've got to stop seeing your husband. And I'm telling you that I'm here. He comes to me. I don't drag him. I don't beg him."

"Don't act so sophisticated. I suppose you didn't call every ten minutes one night when he didn't show up?"

Cookie laughed, shrugging her shoulders. "I suppose I did. That was at first. A woman likes to be sure of her charms. I had given up a perfectly good date to go out with Carlos. It burned me crisp when he didn't show. I was mad, honey. A lot madder than I was hurt."

"All right. If you have so many dates, leave my husband alone." Bernice's voice was cold.

Cookie looked at her. "You mean that, don't you?"

"I never meant anything any more."

"I'm perfectly willing to leave him alone, honey. I don't want to see you upset. Live and let live, that's my motto. There are plenty more where he came from, although you'd probably want to argue that. Tell him to stay away from me. If he'll stay, you have my word. I won't even look at him again."

Bernice cried out, "Pretty sure of yourself, aren't you?"

"O.K., honey. If you won't believe me when I tell you

that I don't particularly want your Carlos, yes. I'm sure of myself. I know that if I want him, I've only got to crook my finger. Yes. But for God's sake, I'm being honest with you. I don't want him. He's pretty. That's all he is. That gets kind of tiresome. It's like a circus. When you've seen it once, you've seen it. If you can make him stay away from me, I'm perfectly pleased."

"Yes. That's what you are saying. But what you mean is that I can't keep him away from you. And as long as I can't, you can afford to be generous."

Cookie sat up on the couch. Her voice was gentle. "You poor dope. You really do love him, don't you? Look. Look, honey. What's your name? Bernice? Look, Bernice, I'm sorry for you. I'm telling you the truth. It isn't even your fault Carlos came running after me. He's what he is. That's all he is. You don't even need to hate yourself. You couldn't have kept him. He would have run after me, no matter what you were. That's Carlos."

"I want him." Bernice's voice cracked. "You've got to let him alone. I beg you."

"Well, don't. Don't beg, Bernice. Begging never kept any man. Don't you understand what I'm telling you? Take your Carlos. Take him away from here. Keep him. I don't care! Do you understand that?"

"I understand just this: You're laughing at me. You're having a swell laugh. Because you know Carlos will come back, and that you'll go on seeing him."

Cookie stood up. "Why don't you go back home, Bernice? This isn't getting us anywhere."

Bernice stood up too. Her face was drained of color. Her flat eyes were distended beneath her glasses.

"I'll kill you, Cookie. If you don't stay away from him, I'll kill you."

Cookie shivered and gathered her negligee closer. "Now you're being silly. I've been trying to tell you, Bernice. You can't kill every woman Carlos chases after. He's a pretty boy. He's got to feel that his beauty is appreciated. It takes new women all the time for that, Bernice. If it wasn't me, it would be some other woman. So what are you going to do?"

Her eyes clouded with tears, Bernice drove the Cadillac

seventy miles an hour along the twisting gulf highway. The first thing she saw clearly was the green community center and the neon sign, "Bar."

She slammed on her brakes, the tires squealing. She tooled the sleek car into the parking place directly before the door of the taproom.

She got out and stalked across the walk. Dugan looked up when she slid onto a stool at the bar.

"Hello, Bernice. Still going at it the slow way?"

"Give me a whisky sour. And don't talk so much."

Dugan looked at her, frowning. "What you mad with me for? I thought you liked for me to talk to you. I figured I knew you pretty well."

She gulped down the drink and shoved the glass back at him. "Yes. You know me. You've known me from the first time I came in here. And that's what I can't understand. Why should you know about me? How do you know what I feel and what I want?"

He fixed her another drink. "It's pretty clear, kid. You want something you're never going to have. And you think you are. And you think you're going to be happy when you get it." He laughed, not looking at her. "Why, I bet you'd even kill if you thought it would mean getting what you wanted."

Bernice slid off the stool. She stood staring at Dugan. "Who are you? What do you know about me?"

Dugan slid the glass of whisky across the gleaming bar. "Relax. I don't know you. It's just that I know anybody that comes here and sits at my bar. I been in this game a long time."

"Why did you tell me that you—you could get me—even poison if I wanted it?"

He shook his head. "I was joking. I was only trying to make you see that you might as well relax and enjoy what you have. I was trying to be funny. I was telling you that you can either make the best of what you got or take the quick, easy way out."

Bernice laughed, shortly at first, then loudly. "I was afraid of you. And all the time it was only because you were telling me the same things I was telling myself."

"Sure. I just hit the nail on the head with you, that's all.

Here, have another drink. This one is on the house. Just because I looked at you and read you right."

Bernice took the whisky sour. She drank it slowly.

She sat on the stool again and leaned across the bar. "You were joking. You were joking about what you could get for me, weren't you?"

"I said I was."

"But I'll bet you could, if you wanted to. If you got enough money for it. Perhaps five hundred dollars."

He swiped at the bar. "Are you trying to get me in trouble, baby?"

Her eyes bored into his. Her voice was cold. "I was only joking."

Their eyes held. "Sure. We're both joking."

"But you could get it, couldn't you?"

He wiped at the bar a long time, putting a lot of muscle behind it. When he looked up, his face was taut. His eyes searched her face. He nodded.

Chapter Seventeen

Bernice prowled the empty cottage.

She glared at the telephone a dozen times. Finally, hating herself, she sank to the chair beside it. She dialed Cookie Dawson's number, sat empty-stomached listening to the wail of the bell across the lines.

"Hello?" Cookie said.

"This is Bernice."

Cookie's voice became hostile. "Yes. What is it, Bernice?"

"I thought you were going to leave him alone. I thought I warned you."

"Look, Bernice. He isn't here. Get that straight. I won't be hounded like this."

"This is only the beginning if you don't leave him alone."

She heard Cookie's indrawn breath. "I know what's the matter with you. I couldn't figure. Now I know. You're crazy. You're just plain crazy, aren't you?"

Bernice laughed. "Why wouldn't I be?"

"Listen to me, Bernice. I don't know where you got my

phone number. But I warn you. Forget it. If you don't stop calling, Bernice, I'll call the police. I mean that. I'm trying to be perfectly calm and perfectly fair with you. But you're giving me a bad case of the creeps. I think you're dangerous."

Bernice laughed again. "For three days you left him alone. Now you've started again. You don't know how dangerous I can be."

"You're wrong, Bernice. I do know. That's why I'll call the police if you don't stop this."

"Why, you stinking little—"

"Look, Bernice. This is the last time I'll ever talk to you. I want you to know that I'm trying to be fair. There's a man here with me. I don't know why I'm doing this. But I want you to listen to me. I think you'll know he isn't your dearly beloved. Here, Joe."

A man's slurring voice poured across the wire. "He'o, li'l ol' Bernice, this here is Joe. Answer to maiden's prayers. You had any maiden's prayers lately, honey? I got answer to 'em."

Suddenly cold, Bernice replaced the receiver. Joe was still talking.

She looked down at her clenched fists. Carlos wasn't with Cookie. What had the little blonde said? If it wasn't Cookie, it would be some other woman.

She got up, trailed into the bedroom. It was one-thirty in the morning. Tiredly she snapped off the lights and fell across the bed. She lay there listening to the boom of the surf, the lonely sounds of cars on the highway, the empty sobbing voices inside her head.

She pushed herself up from the bed and went into the bathroom. She got down the small box of sleeping pills. "Go to a doc," Dugan had told her. "Get some sleeping pills. When you're by yourself, take the pills. Sleep. Pretty soon they won't work any more. But at first they'll work. That's all you care about, ain't it? Right now is the time that matters."

She took three pills, snapped out the light, and returned to her bed.

She toppled across the bed. She lay there, her eyes dry and wide. Silently she prayed for sleep. Maybe with the pills it would be a dreamless sleep. That's what she had to have. She couldn't go on like this, needing sleep, afraid to sleep alone.

The silence stretched taut across the island. She closed her eyes, she pressed the pillow over her face, but she couldn't sleep. Her life moved in slow, hateful scenes like a movie in her mind. The years at Brennan's. The way she'd been plain, unattractive Bernice Harper. All her life. She'd wished herself dead a hundred times to escape her lonely existence. She'd seethed, weeping inside, seeing lovely girls promoted over her, watching helplessly as pretty dumb little things walked away with every man she ever wanted. Plain, colorless Bernice. She remembered the first time she had seen Lloyd. The way the office had whispered that Bernice had been assigned to work with him because he couldn't see her, didn't have to look at her.

She knew now how much he'd loved her. But she still hated him for it. His loving her clearly demonstrated how unwanted she was in the world she longed for. Life with him had been a mockery. Plenty of people were unattractive in one way or another, and plenty were unwanted. But no one ever craved attention and adulation from the people around her as Bernice did. She was starved for it.

How sure she'd been that Lloyd's hidden thousands would buy her what she wanted. Beauty, charm, background—the adulation and attention she desired above everything else in the world.

She lay there, breathless. She could still see the way they had walked along the corridor together. She had run at him, her arms stiff and straight. She could see him falling, slowly toppling away from her, the floor grumbling under her feet as he rolled and twisted to his death without a word of protest.

She was breathing through her opened mouth.

Now in her mind she watched them as they entered Lloyd's old house. Detective, partner, lawyer, doctor, family. The way they believed her when she told her story. They all thought her so plain she would have been joyous at the prospect of being either wife or mistress to Lloyd Deerman. Maybe if she had been lovely, Fred Findlay would have been harder to convince.

She twisted on the bed.

They all knew Lloyd had loved her. There was no mention of her in his will. And she was no insurance beneficiary. She watched their faces as she told her lies. She saw them all believe.

She sat up on the bed, her shoulders slumped round. She had got away with murder. She had that money. But every night she saw Lloyd falling, lying at the foot of the steep stairwell, neck twisted back, sightless eyes fixed on her.

Sure, she had dresses that flattered her figure, and glasses that rendered her blind and gave her headaches. Her hair was trimmed to a halo about her face. Men turned to look at her. She knew she was pretty. She was something turned out by Gloria Soonin's beauty factory. But it ended there.

She had nothing she wanted. She was still starved, still wanting, still lonely. How did they treat lovely women? She still didn't know.

She got up off the bed, trailed across the room. In the gray filmy darkness she could see her reflection in the full-length mirror. The smooth and lovely product of Soonin's Beauty Salon. That's what she saw. A beautiful and synthetic loveliness. But it may as well have been the bitter and unhappy Bernice that stared back at her, the old stringy-haired Bernice. For all Carlos cared, she was the same unwanted Bernice.

She twisted, refusing to look in the mirror any more.

And there, three feet from her, lay Lloyd Deerman! His leg was twisted under him, his head was lolling back on his shoulder. She clapped her hand over her mouth to seal back the scream twisting up through her tightened throat.

She wanted to run but her legs were stiff with paralysis. She could only stand there, feeling herself going completely to pieces inside. Her lips trembled, and she could feel the muscles in her face go taut, pulling down the lower lids of her eyes.

Breath sobbed across her mouth, and she knew she was completely helpless, paralyzed with fright.

She heard the cottage door stealthily opening. Numbed, she stood waiting in the middle of the room. She watched Carlos tiptoe to the bedroom door.

The breath sighed out of her. Her heart began to pump

again, and she was able to drag her legs, and she started toward him.

He gasped, startled at the sight of her moving with cataleptic slowness across the gloom toward him. His head jerked back and he leaped for the side of the door, fighting at the wall switch. Light flooded the room.

Bernice, starkly pale, stood staring at Carlos.

There was terror in his face. Fear had made his eyes wild and round. For a moment they stared at each other.

Slowly Bernice turned and stared at the place where in the darkness she had seen Lloyd's body. She almost laughed aloud. It was her own coat. She'd been angry with Carlos when she'd come in from dinner tonight. She'd carelessly hung up the fur, and it had fallen to the floor.

She wheeled back around, facing Carlos. "Where have you been?" she said.

He looked at her, composure regained. He flattened his tight blond curls with the heel of his hand. "What difference does it make?" he inquired.

"I married you to be near you," she said emptily. "But I never see you at all. You've got to love me, Carlos. I can't stand it if you don't. I swear it—I'll kill myself."

He laughed at her. "Poor little Bernice. Never had anything. No boy friends. No lovers. No wonder. My God, everything is the end of the world with you. I'm afraid to walk in here. You looked like a damned witch standing there in the dark. I thought, so help me God, you were going to stick a knife in me. You wouldn't want to spill my pretty blue blood all over the Rockledge rugs, would you? Inferior grade rugs, baby."

"Stop laughing," she whispered. "You can't go on treating me like this. I won't let you. I won't. I'll die before I'll let you! I'll kill myself!"

He just looked at her, his mouth twisted. "You haven't got the guts," he told her evenly. He pushed past her, trailing the elusive scent of some woman's perfume.

Chapter Eighteen

It was no good. Dozens of nights. Dozens of whisky sours across the bar at Dugan's. Waking in the morning and wondering how she got home at all. Who brought her there? Who put her there? Had the man at the bar beside her really had a face at all? Or was that only Lloyd Deerman having a drink with her? Was that Lloyd Deerman helping her across the highway and pouring her into her lonely bed? Oh, no. That was a dream. The kind of dream you had when you slept.

The nightmares you had now when you were awake. Nothing could stop them. Nothing could still the wailing voices, the intense whispers pleading inside you to die and get it over. You've made a bad bargain and there's only one way out. That's what the voices said. You couldn't escape them. Drink had been an escape. But not any more. There wasn't liquor enough in Dugan's bar to drown the insistent whispering of those bottomless voices.

The drinks in Dugan's weren't strong enough any more. She'd learned to concoct her own whisky sours in the solitary loneliness of her Rockledge Motel cottage. She was preparing one in the kitchenette when the doorbell rang.

It was her sixth drink of the evening and she moved unsteadily across the front room and opened the door.

"Ah, Mr. Rockledge Motel," she said to the owner of the court. "Come in. Come in. Fix you a drink. Know how to fix drinks in a whiffy. Mean jiffy. You'll love it."

"No. No, Mrs. Brandon. Not this evening." The manager looked uncomfortable. "As a matter of fact, you see, I've a kind of unpleasant duty. Don't like to say anything. Like my people to be content as long as they stay here. You folks been here some weeks now. . . ." His voice trailed off.

"Loved it. Loved every god-derned minute of it, Mr. Rockledge Motel. May I call you Rocky? Come in and have a little drinky, Rocky. Got some lovely stuff. Untouched by human humans. You got unpleasant duty. You need a drink."

"No. Really. Some other evening. You see, Mrs. Rawlins—that's my wife—"

"You mean your little ol' name is not Rockledge?"

"Oh, no. I'm George Rawlins. From up in Cedar Rapids. Rawlins is my name. Just called this place Rockledge—"

"Spare me the gory details, Rocky. Can't see why you called this place Rockledge. Haven't even stepped on a bitty stone since I been here. Hasn't kept me from hatin' every minute of it, though."

"Well, that's it. You see, my wife thinks maybe you and your husband might be happier in some other court or hotel."

"What's the matter? We too noisy? We pay you ninety dollars a week, and we too noisy? That's the matter? The sound of my breaking heart too loud, huh? Can't stand the sound?"

"Oh, no. No. Like to have my folks happy. Just with Mr. Brandon coming in all hours, and then noise and lights in your place, why, it disturbs a lot of the other folks. So Mrs. Rawlins said if you could maybe find yourselves a new place by Saturday—"

"The old heave-ho."

"Why, not at all."

"Mounts to same thing. You better come in and have a drink. Maybe she'll be throwing you out next."

Rawlins laughed in a frightened way. "Well, I'm glad you understand. Didn't want any trouble. Hate trouble."

She stepped back. "No trouble. I'll pack my little husband by Saturday. You tell Mrs. Rawlins."

He nodded and hurried away.

For a moment after he was gone, Bernice stood in the center of the room. The world wheeled and whirled about her head. She was sure she was going to start spinning through space. And she thought that would be a good idea. Only she needed one more drink first.

She got a highball from the kitchen and returned to the small front room. She faced herself in the tinted wall mirror. It was no good. Not all the changes she'd made in herself could make Carlos love her.

She finished off the drink, draining the glass. She set the glass down on the table and turning, walked steadily, like someone walking an impossibly straight line, into the bedroom.

She fumbled in the top drawer of her dresser. A smile played about her painted mouth when she came up with her purse. She opened this and scratched inside until she found a small oblong envelope.

She dropped the purse back in the drawer, closed it, and staggered over to the bed. She sat stiffly on the edge of the bed and tore the end off the envelope.

She held it up and shook it. A small red vial plopped out onto the folds of the spread.

She smiled at it. She wondered what was in it. It had cost her almost a thousand dollars. Dugan had looked scared as hell when he'd handed it to her. "Don't come back in here any more," he had said evenly, his face pale. He took her money and shoved it in his pocket without even counting it. "I'm telling you, Bernice, don't come back."

Well, she wasn't coming back. Not any more.

She clutched the red vial in her moist right hand. She got up and marched stiffly back to the front room. She pulled a chair over to where she could watch her made-to-order beauty in that tinted mirror. The whispers were stirring again, a hundred times stronger than ever. But now they were pleasant, and Bernice smiled and kept smiling into that mirror.

She looked about the cottage. The honeymoon cottage. Of course Carlos wasn't here tonight. And of course they were going to be heaved out at the end of the week. But God knew she would be glad to go. She hated the place. And dear Carlos wasn't ever home any more. It was a place of loneliness, a place of bitterness, where she sat and remembered what she had done to Lloyd Deerman, the way she'd shoved him, the way he'd fallen. . . .

And the worst of it was, she'd told herself that if things had been different she could have been happy. If Carlos had loved her, she could have kept Lloyd out of her mind. Now she knew better. You couldn't take a life and live with yourself afterward. No matter what had happened to her, it would have been like this. She couldn't have run fast enough. There was no place far enough. She carried her guilt with her wherever she went.

133

She found a fresh fifth of whisky and a fragile cocktail glass. She kicked a straight chair out of her way as she returned to the mirror. She smiled at her reflection. She'd make her own whisky sour. With red bitters from the little vial.

Whisky had always been an escape. Escape from Carlos' greediness. Escape from the terror of her nightmares. Now death was going to be the final escape.

She snapped the head off the vial. A shocking, pungent odor burned her nostrils. She felt her heart flutter crazily.

She could feel her fingers weaken, trembling as she poured the red stuff into the empty cocktail glass. With a pleased smile at her own forlorn little joke, she tipped in two drops of lemon. She filled it slowly to the brim with amber shadowy liquor.

She stared at the trembling ripples on the surface of the glass. Well, it had been a hell of a short life and a bitter one. Poor, plain little Bernice Harper. She'd killed the man who loved her. She'd taken a life, and now she was going to give one back.

She felt weak in the backs of her knees. Her legs trembled.

"I'm not going to be able to drink it standing up, after all," she said aloud.

She sat down, her knees drawn up, on the ottoman before Carlos' easy chair. Easy chair. Easy. Her bitter eyes raked across his framed photograph. Grinning. Handsome as hell. Cruel as hell. Took everything. Gave nothing in return. Not much longer, my friend.

The liquor winked at her from the cocktail glass.

Suddenly she stood up.

"No!" she said aloud. "He won't have my money. What a damn fool thing I was about to do!"

She crossed the room on shaky legs.

In her bedroom she brought the money from its secret hiding place. Funny, she'd always been able to hide things so no one could find them. Not even Carlos had ever been able to find her money. Now he never would.

She was glad she'd never dared put the money in a bank. She'd been afraid of questions. She feared questions. And the money was always safe enough with her as long as she lived. As long as she kept it hidden from Carlos. And he'd never found her secret hiding place.

She walked stiffly back to her vanity chair.

She met her eyes in the mirror. Her gaze moved to the stacks of money in her hands, and then back to her tear-streaked face, unbrushed hair, dress that was less than her best.

She'd been drinking and that explained the glassiness of her eyes. But the disarray of her hair she couldn't explain at all.

She stacked the money on the vanity before her. She took a long time with creams and lotions and powders on her face, and worked until all the streaks and all the signs of crying were gone. She began to brush her hair, taking careful strokes. The wavelets and curls flipped into place and she had the Soonin halo effect. She grinned, pleased as hell.

She stood up and pulled off the dress, ripping it and letting it fall on the floor at her feet. From her closet she took the most fragile white net evening dress that Elhanner had shown her. She caught her breath, looking at it. The white material rustling in her fingers was almost gossamer. Her underthings weren't nice enough for the dress and she stripped them off, her fingers trembling.

The sheer stockings, the slippers, the white panties and white bra, the white slip were all donned with care and yet with a frantic speed. Bernice didn't even know what compelled her to hurry. The new underthings felt so good against her flesh that Bernice stood still a moment, enjoying the sensual pleasure of their caress. Then she held the dress high over her head, stretching her arms, pulling firm breasts high as the tenuous white netting slid down over her.

She pulled the dress into place, ran the brush once more quickly through her hair. She pirouetted before the mirror, admiring her reflection. They'd done a terrific job. Soonin's. Elhanner. And Carlos. How she'd loved him when he'd been interested in changing her! It had made her love him more than ever. He'd cared and he'd wanted her to look lovely. That's what she thought. He didn't give a damn what she looked like. He didn't give a damn for anything but the green of her money.

She sat down and slowly counted the green flat bills. She was astonished to find that they were already more than half gone.

She looked at them with loathing. Something more than eight thousand dollars. Murder money. What had it bought her? A fast ticket to hell on earth, and nothing else. And she'd been about to die and leave it for Carlos to throw away on his wenches. She was damned if she would!

She giggled, feeling the urge for another drink. She looked at the cocktail, leering up at her. "Oh, no," she said. "I'm not quite ready for you yet."

Weaving as she walked, she got the fifth. She held it up to her mouth and drank lustily. She could feel it burn all the way to her painted toenails. Stars and prisms pinwheeled behind her eyes, and she almost gagged.

Listing slightly, she crossed the room, holding her arms out for invisible supports. From the writing desk she got several large white envelopes. She carried them back to the chair and began stuffing the flat green bills into them.

When they were all sealed, she had a thick stack before her. She got her fountain pen. Scrawlingly, she addressed the envelopes to every charity she could think of. She wrote painfully, pinching the pen in her fingers, squinting through her glamour glasses.

She kept writing until all the envelopes were addressed. Some of the charities were duplicated. She didn't give a damn. Sweat was beaded across her forehead. She threw the pen on the desk. All she cared was that she was keeping Carlos from getting that money.

Smiling her secretive satisfaction, Bernice moved about the room, stuffing the envelopes under books, behind the breadbox in the kitchenette, behind Carlos' grinning photograph. She kept moving until all the letters were hidden.

Sighing expansively, she returned to the ottoman. Sitting down upon it, she looked at the cocktail.

The quick lethal drink. Then she'd call the police. She'd tell them to investigate so they'd find the money addressed to the charities. What a wonderful, bitter joke on Carlos!

She regarded the cocktail. It looked so harmless. She was suddenly afraid she might not have time to call the police after she drank it.

Maybe the pain would be intense. Not that she cared. Still, it might make talking over the telephone impossible.

She got up, went to the telephone. She calmly dialed the police.

"Hello. I want a detective."

"What kind of detective, lady?"

"You got all kinds?"

"Sure. What kind you want?"

"One that can get over here in a hurry. Tell him he better get over to the Rockledge Motel in a hurry. Won't help. Goin' to be too late. But hurry."

"What's your name, sister?"

"Brandon. Bernice Brandon."

"Yeah? What kind of game is this?"

"No time for games, friend. Sorry. You asked me too late. One dance too late. This one is on the house." She repeated her address. The policeman was still sputtering into the telephone. She dropped the receiver back to its cradle.

She walked back to the ottoman. Every step she took made ripples on the surface of her cocktail. She sat down before it.

She reached out her hand. The door opened behind her, and slammed.

Carlos said, "Bernice!"

Chapter Nineteen

She froze. She let her hand sink to her side. She turned on the ottoman, watching Carlos stride into the room.

Tears stung her eyes. He was so handsome. So everything she wanted. She had killed, she had changed her life to have him. She shook her head. Damn him. She'd had nothing she wanted. Living in hell. Married to the devil.

"I need fifty dollars, Bernice."

For a moment she frowned as though she hadn't heard him. Then she began to laugh.

He strode close to her. "Stop that laughing, damn you. You're drunk. I never saw anybody so drunk. Is that the only way you can stand yourself, Bernice?" His laugh was harsh. "Maybe I could stand you if I got drunk enough. Poor, starved little Bernice. Poor, empty little Bernice. Sorry I can't stay and hold your head. I've got a date. I need fifty dollars. Stop laughing and get it for me."

She stopped laughing and stared at him, her face stark. "Get it yourself. I haven't got fifty dollars. It's all gone. You've taken it all. There isn't any more, Carlos. You've had the last penny you're ever going to get from me!"

His voice was a snarl. "I happen to know better. I know about you, Bernice. That blind guy you lived with settled plenty on you before he died. I gambled on that, and that's one time I won. Why do you think I married you?"

"Stop it!" she wailed at him. "Haven't you done enough? You've taken everything from me! Leave me something!"

He looked around the room. His face was white. His mouth pulled wide in a wolfish grin. He said, "Sure, I'll leave you something."

He strode about the room. He jerked open drawers, leaving them open.

Bernice laughed at him through her tears. "You'll have to be quieter. Or did you know? They're throwing us out at the end of the week."

He didn't answer her. He was looking behind the pictures on the wall. They hung crookedly when he moved on. She watched him intently, but a dozen furry images of him moved before her. He ripped the place apart searching for her money. She didn't move from the ottoman. She made no attempt to stop him.

"It's here somewhere!" Carlos rasped. "A checkbook. Something. You've got money, baby, and I'm going to have it."

As he heeled around, his swinging arm knocked over his grinning picture. The envelope toppled to the floor. She sucked in a quick breath and moved a little.

Carlos stared at her. He leaned over and picked up the envelope. She listened to his whoop of laughter when he read the address aloud. He ripped open the envelope and pocketed the money without even counting it.

The room was a shambles when he was through.

As he found each new envelope, he read it gleefully, ripped it open, and stuffed the money in his pockets.

He strode over to her. "So you didn't have any more money, eh, Bernice? So I've taken the last thing from you, have I?" His mouth twisted. "I haven't started to take!"

He grasped up the cocktail she'd fixed for herself. He said mockingly, "Do you mind?"

She opened her mouth to protest.

She closed it. She got up and backed away from him as he drank. She sank against the wall, her hands at her sides, watching him.

She watched him enter hell. His insides cooked, seared, and shriveled, and she could see that in his face. She knew it was happening. His eyes watered. His face was grooved with agony. He began to rail and curse at her. He started toward her, fists doubled. But he didn't make it. Eyes bleak, she watched him twist and stagger and fall at her feet.

Chapter Twenty

Bernice was still staring at him when the police came.
It was a long time before she was aware of them at all. The room filled, at first slowly, and then rapidly like a hopper when the grain spills in too swiftly. There were only the Clearwater police and Mr. and Mrs. Rawlins. Then the county police arrived, and the men from the sheriff's office, the coroner, and the constable. They started talking to her but she continued staring at Carlos' body.

The constable was a heavy, broad-shouldered man with a harried, honest face. He talked with the coroner. He came over to Bernice. "The doctor reports that your husband was poisoned, Mrs. Brandon," he said. "Could you tell us what happened?"

Bernice lifted her head, but she only stared at him, thinking only that her eyes ached.

She let her gaze move about the room. The cottage that had never belonged to her at all now belonged to these strangers, these busy and impersonal men.

They were photographing everything. There was scarcely a moment when there wasn't a bulb flash, the click of shutters. An industrious little man was working with tape measure, pencil, and pad. They were dusting the furniture and taking fingerprints. A detective was questioning Mr. and Mrs. Rawlins. Mrs. Rawlins was sobbing. They might as well close up, she sobbed, and go back to Iowa. They were ruined here. No one would ever come to Rockledge after this awful scandal.

"Don't be silly, lady," the constable said. Bernice stared at him.

"What do you mean?" Mrs. Rawlins sniffled.

"This is the best publicity you could ever get," the constable replied. "Here's a woman who murdered a man. A man with his pockets crammed with money. There's your motive. A clever, scheming woman who used a man and then discarded him. And she lived here at your place."

Everyone in the room was looking at Bernice.

"Sure," said the constable. "They were living pretty royally down here. Cadillac. Ninety bucks a week for this little nest. All the liquor they could drink. There's the money. What happened here tonight? Was this Brandon trying to leave this woman? Is that what happened? He was going to leave her, and he was taking all his money. I think when she starts to talk, that's what she'll tell us." He leaned over Bernice again. "Is that it? He was leaving and you were frantic? Maybe he had some other woman? He had money and you didn't want to share it. You wanted it all. And you killed him for it, didn't you?"

Bernice looked at him. She shook her head.

"You may as well stop lying!" the constable said. "There's the money in his pockets. There's your motive!"

She looked at Carlos, his body twisted on the floor, the money leering at her from his pockets where he had hastily stuffed it. Once she looked at him, she couldn't drag her distended eyes from the agonized face of the only man she'd ever loved. She felt the people about her receding. Their voices sounded a long way off. Her shoulders slumped, her eyes went empty.

The constable stared at her transfixed face. He saw what was happening. He shouted at her. "You did it, sister. You may as well confess."

Bernice could scarcely hear him. She was almost lost to the reality about her. She shook her head.

"Don't think you're the first beautiful woman that's taken a man for everything and then killed him," the constable said.

To Bernice, it was as though she'd been walking slowly and irrevocably away from the sound of his voice. Those words reached faintly after her from a great distance. But they stopped her, pulling her back. She listened, head tilted, waiting.

"—beautiful woman who has killed a man. You think because you're beautiful you can get away with it. You think you can bewitch these people around here, and get away with it. But being beautiful ain't going to get you nowhere. Maybe a lot of publicity at a trial. Maybe a lot of newspaper pictures. Maybe a lot of fools making over you. That's all it'll get you. You did it. You might as well admit it!"

Now she had walked back to him. His words were strong and clear. And Bernice knew that at last she had what she wanted more than anything else in the world—she was going to be treated now the way beautiful women were treated. A little laugh broke across her numbed lips.

The despair washed from Bernice's white face, and a pleased, odd smile replaced it. She looked at the constable, arching her head almost flirtatiously. "Yes," she said. She nodded. "Yes. I did it. Yes, I'm guilty."

THE END

141

BLACK LIZARD BOOKS

JIM THOMPSON
AFTER DARK, MY SWEET $3.95
THE ALCOHOLICS $3.95
THE CRIMINAL $3.95
CROPPER'S CABIN $3.95
THE GETAWAY $3.95
THE GRIFTERS $3.95
A HELL OF A WOMAN $3.95
NOTHING MORE THAN MURDER $3.95
POP. 1280 $3.95
RECOIL $3.95
SAVAGE NIGHT $3.95
A SWELL LOOKING BABE $3.95
WILD TOWN $3.95

HARRY WHITTINGTON
THE DEVIL WEARS WINGS $3.95
FIRES THAT DESTROY $4.95
FORGIVE ME, KILLER $3.95
A MOMENT TO PREY $4.95
A TICKET TO HELL $3.95
WEB OF MURDER $3.95

CHARLES WILLEFORD
THE BURNT ORANGE HERESY $3.95
COCKFIGHTER $3.95
PICK-UP $3.95

ROBERT EDMOND ALTER
CARNY KILL $3.95
SWAMP SISTER $3.95

W.L. HEATH
ILL WIND $3.95
VIOLENT SATURDAY $3.95

PAUL CAIN
FAST ONE $3.95
SEVEN SLAYERS $3.95

FREDRIC BROWN
HIS NAME WAS DEATH $3.95
THE FAR CRY $3.95

DAVID GOODIS
BLACK FRIDAY $3.95
CASSIDY'S GIRL $3.95
NIGHTFALL $3.95
SHOOT THE PIANO PLAYER $3.95
STREET OF NO RETURN $3.95

HELEN NIELSEN
DETOUR $4.95
SING ME A MURDER $4.95

DAN J. MARLOWE
*THE NAME OF THE GAME
IS DEATH* $4.95
NEVER LIVE TWICE $4.95

MURRAY SINCLAIR
ONLY IN L.A. $4.95
TOUGH LUCK L.A. $4.95

AND OTHERS . . .
FRANCIS CARCO • *PERVERSITY* $3.95
BARRY GIFFORD • *PORT TROPIQUE* $3.95
NJAMI SIMON • *COFFIN & CO.* $3.95
ERIC KNIGHT (RICHARD HALLAS) • *YOU PLAY THE BLACK
AND THE RED COMES UP* $3.95
GERTRUDE STEIN • *BLOOD ON THE DINING ROOM FLOOR* $6.95
KENT NELSON • *THE STRAIGHT MAN* $3.50
JIM NISBET • *THE DAMNED DON'T DIE* $3.95
STEVE FISHER • *I WAKE UP SCREAMING* $4.95
LIONEL WHITE • *THE KILLING* $4.95
THE BLACK LIZARD ANTHOLOGY OF CRIME FICTION
Edited by **EDWARD GORMAN** $8.95

HARDCOVER ORIGINALS:
LETHAL INJECTION by **JIM NISBET** $15.95
GOODBYE L.A. by **MURRAY SINCLAIR** $15.95

Black Lizard Books are available at most bookstores or directly from the
publisher. In addition to list price, please send $1.00/postage for the
first book and $.50 for each additional book to **Black Lizard Books, 833
Bancroft Way, Berkeley, CA 94710.** California residents please include
sales tax.